Frans Oskar Wågman

SHERLOCK HOLMES
IN A NEW LIGHT

Sherlock Holmes in a New Light
by Frans Oskar Wågman
First published as
"Sherlock Holmes i ny belysning"
by Wahlström & Widstrand, Stockholm, 1908
Translated and edited by Mats Ingelborn
This edition Copyright © 2024
Cover by Mats Ingelborn with
illustration from LeoEdition/Shutterstock
ISBN print: 978-91-89822-91-7
ISBN e-book: 978-91-89822-92-4
Published by Yabot AB, Stockholm, Sweden, 2024

FOREWORD

DEAR Reader,
In your hands you hold a remarkable piece of early Swedish detective fiction. Published in 1908 under the pseudonym Sture Stig, "Sherlock Holmes in New Light" was written by Frans Oskar Wågman (1849-1913), a Swedish priest and author who pioneered the detective parody genre in Sweden.

The book presents a series of stories framed as confidential revelations made by Dr. John Watson to a visiting Swedish priest in England. Through Sture Stig's telling, we discover these "flat cases"—the failures that the great detective would prefer to forget.

Here we encounter a different Sherlock Holmes: one whose logical mind is outmaneuvered by female cunning, and whose rational facade crumbles when confronted with what appears to be his own double. We even witness the notorious Professor Moriarty succeeding in outsmarting the master detective.

Yet Holmes is not the only character cast in an unfamiliar light. Dr. Watson emerges as a complex figure, caught between admiration for and jealousy of his famous friend. His marriage suffers under the strain of midnight ventures through London's questionable districts, and we glimpse the frustrations of a man who feels perpetually resigned to a supporting role in his own life story.

Though satirical in nature, these stories offer both cleverly constructed mysteries and a masterful pastiche of Arthur Conan Doyle's style. Among genre enthusiasts, Wågman's works have long held the status of classics.

For this new edition, I have carefully updated the language to make these entertaining tales accessible to contemporary readers while preserving their Victorian atmosphere and Wågman's distinctive wit.

Allow yourself to be drawn into these hidden treasures of the Holmes canon, where the familiar world of 221B Baker Street appears in an entirely fresh and unexpected light.

Happy reading!

Mats Ingelborn

1. SHERLOCK HOLMES IN EVERYDAY LIFE

During my last stay in England, I made several interesting acquaintances, but none so fascinating as that of Dr Watson.

Who in their right mind would not know his name? The schoolboy in the third grade, who has never heard of Charlemagne and may think Goethe was a coppersmith, knows who Dr Watson is. Yet he is not one of those great fixed stars that light up a whole world with their glow. He's just a small planet orbiting and drawing light from a brilliant sun: Sherlock Holmes. The world-famous Sherlock Holmes, the Napoleon of detectives, the Aristotle of analytical reasoning, the enchantment of all sensation seekers, the idol of schoolboys, the terror and admiration of criminals. Homer sang the praises of the Trojan heroes, and Thiers won his honour as Napoleon's historian - Watson is Sherlock Holmes Homer and Thiers. That is his greatness.

Imagine my delight when I met the doctor as a guest at a country house where I had been invited to spend a few days! Of course, I tried to talk with him about his famous friend and master, but for a long time in vain. He was like a well-fortified castle. It was only on the afternoon of the second day that I got him to surrender. I crept up on him where he was sitting alone in a beer hall, whose only exit I blocked, and said:

"Now, Doctor, you must tell me something about your friend Sherlock Holmes."

"About Holmes?" he repeated as indifferently as if the name belonged to his shoeshine boy.

"Yes, about the man whose genius and life you vividly portrayed in your books."

"We could talk about something more pleasant on a beautiful summer day like this."

"Can anything be more pleasant than talking about a friend and great man?" I asked, almost irritably, adding, "Almost living with him."

"Live with Holmes yourself for three whole years, as I have done, and then tell me if you find it agreeable!" I was quite taken aback by the excited tone in which the doctor uttered the words.

"What do you mean, Doctor? Did you not find the well-known residence at 221B Baker Street ideal?"

"I will confide in you. People have wondered why I married head over heels - see my book 'The Sign of the Four' - without a penny to my name and practice. But you see, I only did it to get away from Baker Street."

My face formed a big question mark. But I didn't have to open my mouth to get an answer. The doctor's tongue resembled those huge machine wheels that are so difficult to get going but can hardly be stopped.

"You wonder what it was like on Baker Street," he continued. 'I'll tell you in one word: filthy. I won't mention the stains on carpets, furniture, and wallpaper, which result from Holmes's constant experiments with acids and liquids. I will only mention the visits of his volunteer detective corps of boys, who two or three times a week delivered samples of all the different kinds of street dirt to be found in our capital, which is so richly blessed with this substance."

"Of course, quite unpleasant," I admitted.

"However, there were worse things. I realise that I never had any peace. During the constant visits of clients, I had to serve time as a witness and historiographer, and from time to time, I had to accompany them on nocturnal reconnaissance. I could have put up with this anyway, but Holmes's squeaking on the violin, sometimes through the night - no, no nerves in the world could cope with that. When it was going on, it chased sleep away, and when it stopped, you could hear it both awake and asleep for weeks."

"I have read in your books that Mr. Holmes's handling of his instrument was a little peculiar," I thought I should say.

"Strange? Say infernal. One night, he spent four hours playing two notes, slowly and gloomily, always on the same two notes. If I hadn't taken chloral, I'm sure I would have gone mad. But still, this ordeal was small compared to another. You know from the books that Holmes has an incredible ability to change his appearance, face, gait, voice, and whole being, and this not only with the help of an actor's props but also by his pure mimicry. In an instant, before your very eyes, he became a completely different person. But it was not at all uplifting, for example, to sit down to dinner with your friend Holmes opposite you, and then, after you had spent two seconds on the mutton roast, find yourself sitting opposite a broad-mouthed, half-idiot cabman or a very drunken bargeman. That doesn't make for an appetite or a pleasant dining experience. If he had transformed into a fine lady, a beautiful actress, or a handsome housekeeper, I would not have said anything, but he never did. He always drew his characters from the seedier strata of society. Nor was it more pleasant, while enjoying your evening pipe with several 'The Lancet,' to see a boxer come in and start a fight or to wake from your sweetest sleep at a sudden flash of light and have an Irish labourer with red hair, one eye bruised and the other covered by a blindfold standing before your bed. Of course, it was usually Holmes, but you could never be sure. You never knew whether it was him or someone else; that was the unpleasant part. Usually, it was him, but not always. One afternoon, I was sitting alone, half-asleep, sipping a grog, when a salesman came creeping in, as quiet as a cat. At seeing me, he stopped at the door in embarrassment, but irritated by Holmes' antics, I exclaimed: 'No, Holmes, you're not fooling me this time. I recognise you despite the disguise.' Holmes seemed struck by my interruption, went into the next room, came out briefly, and left without saying goodbye. But this time, it was not Holmes, but a stranger from the street who, to commemorate the visit, brought with him a gold watch, a nickel writing stand - he thought it was silver, of course - and a collection of picks from Holmes's rich assortment. We never caught up with the chap."

　　　　　　　　　　　　

The doctor finally made a break that I felt obliged to fill in.

"Undoubtedly, all this causes discomfort, but Doctor, you have been compensated by witnessing and participating in your friend's world-famous exploits."

The doctor blew out a cloud of smoke with disdainful energy. "You think so? Then sit for two or three hours crouched on your heels behind a box in a pitch-black rat hole of a cellar vault, waiting for bandits who would have no more compunction about sending half a dozen revolver bullets through your body than they would about killing a mosquito. Then tell me if you will not decline both the honour and the pleasure. Admittedly, there was some excitement in this, but the experiments were at Baker Street! For example, the one where Holmes analysed all kinds of cigarette ash. In five days, we both smoked 400 cigars. Can you imagine the state of the body after such a mad enterprise? The rooms were so full of smoke that when we opened the windows, whole clouds billowed out. Passers-by sensed a fire and alerted the fire brigade, and only after they drowned both us and our laboriously collected ash samples in a river of water was the mistake discovered."

"Well, that's the worst I've heard," I added.

"The worst!" the doctor exclaimed. "Of course not! The poison experiments were worse. During them, one walked in constant agony. Who was to say that Holmes did not spill a few grains of strychnine on his cuff and then drop them in his food, or that a dose of hashish was not slipped into his tobacco because Holmes wanted to study its effect on a human being - like every great scientist, he had no qualms about making scientific progress. One day, he got up to an unpleasant business. We stayed for the summer in a small villa we had rented by the coast. My friend showed me a collection of small, well-corked glass tubes: 'Look here, Watson, I have the means in my hands to poison all London and Sussex and Kent besides. 'This is "Zum-Zum," the most potent poison in the world, almost invisible and finer than the finest dust. A tenth of a milligram of it inhaled into your nose or mouth, Watson, will make you as stiff as the statue of Nelson in two minutes, and no doctor in England could save your life. But there is a Nemesis; even his smile would disappear.

In the afternoon, I sat idly by the window, staring out over the meadow that sloped slowly towards the sea. I heard my friend busying himself in his room and going out of the verandah door, and soon, I saw him striding across the meadow. But his gait had nothing of the gait of an ordinary man, let alone of his swift and confident one. He advanced like an undertaker in his wife's funeral procession, like an Indian scout in the neighbourhood of the enemy's camp, like a gouty man on a floor strewn with nails. I was surprised, but soon my surprise grew to astonishment. Up on a small bare rock, Holmes stopped and - excuse me for making my account a little intimate! - pulled off his trousers, not like you and me in the evenings with a few manly jerks but as gently and slowly as if they were his skin. Then he lit a couple of matches, set fire to the garment and carefully fuelled the fire with paper and dry moss. Imagine the sight I saw: my friend up on the hillside in his hat and jacket but without trousers, his white underwear fluttering lightly in the wind and the mysterious fire illuminating his strange figure! He must have gone mad. I rushed out and tried to approach him, but he pulled his revolver out of his pocket, pointed it at me and shouted: 'Keep away, Watson, 100 metres away, or I'll shoot you! The tone of his voice told me he was serious. When the fire consumed the last of his trousers, Holmes made his way to the house, still keeping me at a distance with his revolver; after that, he set to work in a manner that did nothing to increase my conviction that his brain was in balance. He went to every open window and set fire to the curtains, threw burning papers on the summer-dry cardboard roof, and made little fires in the verandah and at every corner of the house. Within ten minutes, the building was in full flame; within half an hour, it was a blazing sea of fire, and when people from the sparsely populated neighbourhood gathered to put out the fire, all they had in front of them was a smoking and glowing pile of ashes.

Only now did Holmes put the revolver in his pocket and beckon me to come. 'Do you understand this, Watson? Of course, I don't. So listen! During my experiments with 'Zum-Zum,' I accidentally dropped the tube of poison. It broke against my trouser leg and the floor, and both were contaminated with the dangerous substance that only fire can destroy. I did what I did to prevent the spread of the poison and the accidents caused by it. It will be an expensive business for me: £1,000 for the villa and 22 shillings for the trousers, but - his face took on a delighted expression here - 'I now know all the properties of Zum-Zum at the bottom, and nobody in the world does it more than I.' Holmes is an egotist; have you noticed? He took his trousers into account, but he didn't consider my entire summer wardrobe, which had burned up. Holmes is a great egotist."

The doctor had got so far in his descriptions when, to my great disappointment, the ladies of the manor arrived and interrupted the interesting stories, and I did not manage all evening to get the doctor alone and in the mood to continue. But I am an optimist and hope for tomorrow.

My hopes were not dashed. At breakfast, the doctor and I were invited to participate in a big rabbit hunt on the moors. Since my military service, I have hardly touched a gun, but when I saw that the doctor was going to be there, I was happy to accept the offer. I had my quarry to hunt.

Soon, the burnt heath was dotted with red and green patches—hunters' outfits. The dogs barked, and the shots clattered like hail against a tin roof. I was pleased to find that the doctor's interest in hunting was as little as mine, and after an hour, he sat down on a rock to light his pipe. I had always kept close to him, and now I took my place at his side.

"You're not homicidal, Doctor," I began.

"No - it - is - I - not," he replied, pausing between each word with sharp puffs from his clogged pipe.

"No wonder," I began my attack. "Anyone involved in hunting the world's most dangerous criminals must despise today's prey."

"I hate rabbit meat," said the doctor dryly.

So, my first attack was repelled. I had to try a roundabout movement.

"They shoot well, those ones," I said, pointing to the hunters. "They don't miss."

"They shoot well," the doctor replied briefly.

"They look like your friend, Sherlock Holmes. He never escaped his prey."

"Didn't it?" The doctor became more animated. "Yes, it did."

"But in the books..."

"The books," interrupted the doctor, as contemptuously as if he harboured the Caliph Omar's feelings for them, "the books! You don't tell everything you know in them. Most things are kept quiet if they don't fit in. Above all, a biographer does that. How many historians of England have mentioned that Richard the Lionheart was afraid of rats? Which painter has portrayed Queen Elizabeth with black teeth, even though hers were really black?"

"You amaze me," I said. "I have learnt from your books that the official police always get lost, but that the great Sherlock Holmes could make a mistake and be fooled is incomprehensible, incredible."

"Is it? If I've said A, why don't I also say B and give reasons for my opinion?"

And the doctor told us, as the sun beat down on our backs and the rifle shots rang out further and further away on the moor.

2. The Archer affair

MY wife had travelled to a health resort. As usual on such occasions, I visited Sherlock Holmes at my old home in Baker Street.

Neither of us, however, was particularly sociable at the moment. Uninterested, I was hunched over a book. At the same time, Holmes, without uttering a word, sat in his armchair with his eyes closed and his violin between his knees, expressing the disharmony of his soul through music.

For three hours, I had put up with the ear-splitting noise - the habit is second nature - but eventually, the suffering became overwhelming.

"Don't grind so infernally on that torture device," I pleaded in as friendly a tone as I could manage under the circumstances.

Holmes looked up in surprise. "I thought you loved music, Watson."

"Yes, but not that. I know nothing like it, except the lamentation of the Mbogo people at the bier of their chief, or the evening concert of five starving hyenas in the Sahara Desert."

"It is, however, the expression of my present mood," Holmes replied meekly, "and according to recent theories of art, every expression is beautiful, so long as it is true. You are aesthetically behind, Watson; you are not keeping up with the times. My music is a little jarring because my soul is unbalanced. My intelligence is wasting away because it has no problems to solve, problems worthy of me, problems that border on the impossible. I perish from idleness."

"Have you nothing to do, Holmes? No investigations?"

"Almost nothing. In a whole week, only two murders, an attempted poisoning, three burglaries, a bank robbery - almost nothing, especially nothing to satisfy the needs of my intellect."

"But I think..."

"It's nothing to a brain constructed like mine." He sighed. "Our time is degenerate; intelligence is in decline."

"Oh, we have a lot of great men, statesmen, artists, poets, inventors: Edison, Ibsen, Marconi, Chamberlain..."

"Bah, what kind of intelligence does it take to be this? At least no original intelligence. To be a poet, what is that? Borrowing old thoughts and dressing them up in new expressions. Inventor? To be able to exploit the vagaries of chance. A statesman? No one accuses the statesmen of our time of genius or greatness, so I can leave them out of the equation. A composer? Count the keys on the piano, Watson, and you will see that there are really only 12 notes. Composing is putting three or three of them together. A child should be able to do that. No, there are only two tasks in our time that require a developed intelligence: committing crimes and solving crimes. These require originality, imagination, psychology, knowledge, logic, and, above all, logic. But even in this field, the number of geniuses is decreasing; there are now only two."

"Of which you are one, Master."

"Yes, and my brother Mycroft, the other. But even our intellectual faculties wither for lack of stimulation."

I was about to politely object when we heard a carriage stop outside the house. The doorbell rang, and heavy steps climbed the stairs.

"A client, Watson," Holmes exclaimed intuitively, and at that moment, the visitor entered.

He was a short man, conspicuously obese, with grey hair and a face that was too red. The nose, in particular, would have gained in appearance if its colour had been more consistent with nature's original. The man's attire was not overly modern and was worn with little originality, but it was precious and well-groomed: a diamond shone in his shirtfront, and a thick gold chain circled his stomach.

"Mr Sherlock Holmes, I presume?" he asked in a slightly hoarse voice.

"Quite right," my friend replied. "Please sit down!"

"I recognised you from the book description," the stranger announced.

"The whole world knows me," said Holmes simply. "This is my friend Dr Watson."

The stranger bowed to me. "Of course, I should have realized it; yes, I should. When visitors come to see you, Mr Holmes, the doctor, always sits in that armchair. It says so in the books - my son Jim has them all, and I've read quite a few. The doctor always sits in the armchair. It never fails. My name is Benjamin Perkins Archer..."

"50 years old," Holmes interjected.

"51, just turned," Archer corrected.

"It doesn't matter," Holmes made a dismissive motion with his hand. "You have come here in a hansom cab."

"True, but..."

"You live outside London."

"Ah, Mr Holmes, you've noticed my muddy shoes. Excuse me..."

"Don't bother with excuses! You live a life without chores."

The man's eyes went wide. "You're right."

"You are a friend of a good dinner, a juicy roast beef, a fat salmon."

"You amaze me, sir."

"You like a glass of old port with your meal, and you like to nap in your armchair with a bottle next to you on the table."

"But how on earth, sir, do you know..."

"I know all I wish to know. You come here seeking my counsel while groping in the dark."

"Quite right, sir."

"You are threatened by a danger or loss."

Archer jerked in his chair. "You know that too, Mr Holmes? I fear it is so. Are you omniscient then, sir?"

"Not exactly. It's not a person. You are a businessman."

"No, I'm not."

"Then your father was?"

"No, he was a bell ringer at St Stephen's parish in Clipton."

"Strange," my friend muttered to himself. "Than your uncle?"

"In a way. He was the second bailiff of Tugadore in India."

"Good," said Holmes. "Let me tell you something, Mr. Archer: you have mistaken your calling; you should have been a businessman. Nature has made you for it."

With his whole fat face shining with pleasure, Archer grabbed my friend's hand and squeezed it warmly. "You don't say, sir! You don't know how happy you make me with that. When I was a boy, I always wanted to work in a grocer's or a wine shop, but my father objected; it did not suit his half-priestly calling, he thought. He was always so strict about what was appropriate."

"He made a mistake, but it's human to err. But let's get to the point. First, your antecedentia, if you please."

Archer began to talk. As was his habit, Holmes listened with his eyes closed and his fingers playing some invisible instrument.

"My antecedents?" Archer began. "Well, gentlemen, I will give them as honestly as I had sworn on the Bible. As I said, my father was a bell-ringer in Clipton - a respectable but unprofitable occupation. I was an only child and was apprenticed as a potter, eventually becoming master of my own workshop and marrying Sally Creeks, a beautiful woman when she was young - but beauty fades, gentlemen - a splendid woman, I can say that over her grave, though the mood was a little difficult - well, that is always the case with the weaker sex, so I do not mean that as a criticism. You are what you are made of. My profession was good for a while, especially during the years when the fascination with antiques in the ceramics industry was at its peak. I had the reputation of being the foremost maker of Assyrian and ancient Persian clay pots - no one else got the right, unadorned shape of the decorations as I did. I had my clientele among the finest antique dealers in England, and without boasting, I can say that several of my works occupy a prominent place in the antiquities museums of Europe. But Sally died, the business started to go downhill, and eventually it collapsed."

"Brandy and whisky," Holmes muttered half aloud.

"Perhaps you are right, sir," Archer admitted good-naturedly. "Man is a weak vessel, gentlemen, and because of my profession, I can speak of it with some expertise."

Holmes nodded in agreement. "Go on!"

"I then became a police officer in Brushy upon Trent. For three years, I held the post, but certain circumstances..."

"Brandy and whisky," my friend interjected, but Archer pretended not to hear and continued:

"...forced me to leave it. After a while, I was put in charge of bottle rinsing at a brewery. The work was not unpleasant, but the pay was small, and the premises were poor; nevertheless, I held out until three years ago, when I left the job because of..."

"Brandy and whisky."

"No, sir, you are really doing me an injustice - because of the Indian heritage."

"The Indian heritage!" Holmes opened his eyes, and his expression took on the likeness of a hound dog sniffing out big game. "Ah! An Indian heritage! Pay attention, Watson, a new Agra treasure! You are a most interesting man, Mr. Archer. Get on with it! As many details as possible!"

"Oh, there's not much to say about the inheritance, though it was timely enough, and I'm glad of it. As I was saying, gentlemen, I had an uncle of whom I knew little, except that people who had been in India told me that he had a post as a bailiff out there and was quite rich. He was married to a native woman, a washerwoman, some said; others said she was a coloured princess who had brought enormous wealth. Some knew that they had lived together as lovebirds, others that she had been hanged for attempting to murder her husband. Still others took a middle course and said that they had begun as doves and ended as hyenas, and they probably came closest to the truth - such is the way of the world. I was never told if they had children. They said yes and no, and I didn't think it was any of my business either. You see, gentlemen, I never had any thought of inheritance. The news that my uncle had bequeathed me his entire fortune, £30,000, came upon me like a bolt from the blue, a very pleasant one indeed, especially as I had been dismissed from the brewery on account of... no, Holmes, not brandy and whisky as you are about to say - they had nothing to do with it, it was the beer. But now I could give the brewery up in good humour, and I bought myself a farm out at Brightstone, and there I live quietly, comfortably, and independently on my interest."

"Go on!" Holmes encouraged.

"Money," resumed Mr Archer, "is unpleasant when you have not got it, but if you have plenty of it, it is very good. I am now as happy a man as any, enjoying every possible comfort, having no cares, and no lack of reputation in my neighbourhood. Gentlemen invite me to dinner, and I am elected a member of both the church and school councils. I have reason to believe that Miss Ellinor, the sister of a Member of Parliament, would not refuse to be Mrs Perkins Archer number two, but, gentlemen, I beg your pardon! The fox that lost one paw in the scissors will not stick the other. No new edition of Sally, no stepmother for my son Jim! He's 13 years old, tall, and a very handsome boy, a gentleman. His school is at Walkers-house, where only children of standing are admitted, and he is close friends with young Robert Stanton, son of Sir Edward Stanton of Rawnbury-hill and cousin to his lordship Lord Markland and Colonel Forth of the Hussars. The boys are like clay and long straw, and Jim is present on a couple of days' visit to Rawnbury-hill. There, he is as good as a child in the house."

"I have met the Colonel at a sporting contest, and have had the honour of giving his lordship my advice on an awkward occasion," remarked Holmes respectfully. "Go on!"

"So, I was as calm and pleasant as I could wish until yesterday, when something happened that completely took away both my sleep and my appetite."

"Tell me, Mr Archer. You are very interesting."

"I had my dinner alone yesterday, because the boy was with his friend Bob, son of Sir..."

"We know your son's friend, don't dwell on his family connections, sir."

"Well, I'd had my dinner and was just sitting considering an important municipal question, whether or not to charge a toll at the new bridge - Sir Edward wants it, but the Vicar objects - when I decided to look up a map in the library - I've set one up at Brightstone Park. I made my way through the corridor, and in doing so - gentlemen, shall I call it luck or bad luck? - I accidentally tripped on the carpet..."

"Brandy and whisky..."

"No, sir! If anything, it was old port - but anyway, I stumbled, and suddenly I was lying straight on the floor with my arms outstretched, as if I wanted to embrace the iron stove. When I got up, I was holding a crumpled piece of paper in my right hand - it had been thrown behind the stove, and in the fall, I had unconsciously grabbed it. I am a tidy person, gentlemen, and I like my house to be tidy. I am particularly annoyed by papers lying around. I thought I would give the maid a good scraping, so I took the paper with me as proof of her carelessness. In the library, I happened to glance at it, and, gentlemen, if I am not mistaken, it is a case of some terrible offence."

My friend, Holmes' eyes, took on a phosphorescent sheen.

"Where do you have the paper?" he asked.

"Here," replied Archer. "That is why I have sought you out, sir."

Holmes scrutinised the paper for three or four minutes, examined it with a magnifying glass, held it to the light of day and smelled it. Then he handed it to me.

It was oblong, square, badly wrinkled and not very clean. About a quarter of its upper right part was torn off. What I read was the following:

"Wednesday 22 ..... day of venge ... tomorrow .... finished ..... second popp .... no revol ... ... ly dagger and forgi ....ld man sleeps at 10 o'clock? .... rd door on the right .... in coridor? The Labourer of the night."

When I returned this curious document to my friend's hands, he spoke in his methodical way:

"We note that the paper is of the ordinary, cheap variety, without anything distinctive; it is apparently a leaf from a notebook. We further note that it is a letter, part of which has been torn off. We then have to restore its wording to its unstamped state. Have you done so, Mr. Archer?"

"Of course not! How could I?"

"Then I will do it. Only two things cause some difficulty; one is the date. The day is the 22nd, but the month? What month, Mr. Archer?"

"No one can know; the month's name has been cancelled."

"Oh, the matter is simple enough. The letter is not old; I can safely say it was written this year, and the ink is not completely blackened. Take this almanac, Mr Archer, and see how many Wednesdays this year have dates of the 22nd!"

Archer leafed through the little book. "Well, my soul, never have I seen the like! It's only a -Wednesday the 22nd of August."

"And today is Thursday the 23rd," said Holmes gravely. "The letter speaks of a crime to be committed tonight."

I saw Archer shudder, but Holmes continued in his calm, methodical way, which seemed so impressive:

"The first riddle is solved; the second we leave for now. I will fill in the other small gaps and read as follows: Wednesday 22 August. The day of vengeance is tomorrow. Everything is ready. Meet me at the second poplar. No revolver, only dagger and - here comes the enigmatic word which we will skip for now - The old man sleeps at 10 o'clock? Isn't his bedroom the third door on the right in the corridor? Mr Archer, are there any poplars at Brightstone Park?"

"Sure, a whole avenue."

"Good. And your bedroom is..."

"Third door on the right in the corridor!" Archer exclaimed in horror. "Good heavens! Is it really me?"

"It seems so. When do you go to bed?"

"Early, already at nine."

"And so sleeps at ten o'clock."

"I'm unhappy! 'The old man' - is that really me?"

"Absolutely."

"They want to steal my money."

"They want something worse, sir. They want to take revenge on you and use daggers."

"And this would happen to me tomorrow?"

"No, in the night ahead. But you may rest assured. You have placed your cause in my hands, and not a hair of your head shall be harmed."

"Mr Holmes, you are my guardian angel."

"You will be as safe tonight as you are now, sitting in my armchair. But let us proceed with our investigation. Who is the letter writer?"

Despite his pleas, both Archer and I had to leave the question unanswered. Holmes smiled a little superiorly.

"We'll sort that out together. The large, naively shaped letters suggest a hand that is not too used to handling the pen, but they are not written by a completely uneducated person either. The style is not that common among us Englishmen, but similar to that used by someone who is learning our language and writing. Then there are two spelling mistakes: 'poplar' with two P:s and 'corridor' with only one R. I therefore have seven different but plausible hypotheses; for reasons you will realise later, I choose this one: the letter writer is a foreigner. But of what nationality? Not a European; such a one uses in our days neither the word nor the thing 'dagger' - he would say 'knife.' This circumstance, however, would not be a sufficient reason for my assumption, but it is decisively confirmed by the word in the letter we have passed over so far. That word is, of course, 'poisoned' and refers to some weapon, but no European, however great a scoundrel he may be, uses poisoned weapons for the simple reason that he does not understand appropriate poisons. So the writer of the letter is a non-European, but from what country? He feels he has reason to take revenge on you, Mr Archer. Have you ever insulted a Japanese, a Chinese, an African, or any such foreigner?"

"None at all, as far as I know."

"You are a wiser man than you realise, sir; you are telling the whole truth. It is someone whom you have unwittingly offended. Have you no idea who?"

"Not a bit."

"I will tell you, but first, I have a question. Does your uncle's estate contain any precious, peculiar gems or the like?"

"Not a single one. The inheritance consisted only of securities and bonds."

"That simplifies things considerably. We are not dealing with any Brahmins or other fanatics who have come here to recover the stolen eye of the god Vishnu or any such thing. No one can mistake the person of the letter writer: he is your Indian cousin, the son of your uncle, and the Indian woman. You, Mr. Archer, have received the inheritance he regards as his rightful property; he wants revenge and perhaps to recover what he can from the inheritance."

"You are right, sir! It is quite clear: it is my Indian cousin." Mr Archer was beside himself with admiration, and I, too, had to say a few flattering words about my friend's acumen.

Holmes smiled quietly. "If you had any logic, my friends, you would have come to this conclusion yourself. After all, you received the inheritance three years ago."

"Two and three-quarters years ago, to be precise."

"That confirms it. Your Indian cousin did not decide to take revenge immediately. The preparations for the journey took time, and even more, the journey itself. Once here, he had to familiarise himself with the conditions, the customs, the facts, and the language, the latter because he needed English helpers. You may object that he was the son of an Englishman and had an English upbringing, but it is clear that his father did not care for him in the least, since he did not leave him a penny in his will. If you still think that two or three years is too long a period, I would ask you to remember that an Easterner is patient; he does not hurry; he wants to be sure that the blow is struck before he delivers it."

"You are a wonderful man, Mr Holmes!" Archer exclaimed enthusiastically. "It's no wonder my son Jim is crazy about the books about you. To think, an hour ago, neither you nor I had any idea that my Indian cousin existed, and now we know exactly what sort of person he is."

Holmes nodded in favour and agreement. "We now come to the addressee of the letter. Here we have the following facts to consider: the addressee is in your house; he or she - the sex I leave undecided for the present, but use the masculine form for convenience - has been disturbed in reading the letter, and has thrown it behind the stove; he has access to your apartment; he is a thoughtless and frivolous person - no one but such a person throws such a letter away, even with the intention of taking it up later; he has the task of cleaning the corridor. Otherwise, he must fear that someone else, sweeping or otherwise, might find and read the letter; he has been prevented from collecting it before and during dinner because you found it just as you left the table. In my opinion, the recipient is undoubtedly a 'she,' a feminine being. Is there anyone in your household to whom this applies, Mr Archer?"

"It's Mary. I can swear it's Mary."

"And who is Mary?"

"The first maid, a lively and thoughtless girl. She cleaned upstairs, and in the corridor, I had the dining room door open for warmth during dinner. It's her and no one else."

"Possible, even likely. However, we will probably find out later."

"It is she, the vile creature, who wants to murder me! And I have been so kind to her! But I will have her arrested..." Archer had sprung to his feet and stood in his rage, bold and strong as the image of Mars. But he sank back into his chair, utterly disheartened by Holmes's heavily accented address:

"No, sir, you shall not. Arrest her, or say but a word to her, and the real culprit will be warned and will retire for the present, but make new plans against you, which will not, as now, by chance fall into your hands. It is the Indian cousin whom it is important to catch; only when he is behind bars, or banished from England, can you sleep safely."

"What am I supposed to do?" Archer complained.

"Nothing, absolutely nothing. Go home, have your dinner, and drink your wine - though today in very small quantities - read your newspaper and go to bed as usual at nine."

"And let me be murdered like a woodchuck in its nest!" Archer exclaimed in horror.

"When I, Sherlock Holmes, have taken care of the matter, you will be as safe as a king in his castle, guarded by a whole army. You must obey me blindly or stand your ground alone; which will you choose?"

"I obey, sir; I obey like a blind puppy. But you will come with me now to Brightstone Park?"

"No, that would attract attention and spoil my plans. But don't worry. The moment I am needed, I shall be there. Listen, Mr. Archer, where are the kitchen and the servants' quarters?"

"At the west end of the house, lower floor."

"Which rooms on the east side?"

"A flower room and a living room."

"The corridor is upstairs?"

"Sure."

"Can you make sure that the hooks for the windows in the living room are not attached tonight? But nobody must notice anything."

"I can easily organise that without drawing attention to myself, because I usually make sure that the windows and doors are properly closed every night."

"That's good."

"Excuse me, Mr. Holmes, but I wanted to mention that from the living room, a spiral staircase leads up to the corridor. Perhaps it might be useful for you to know."

"You do not lack judgement, Mr Archer. Your enlightenment saves me trouble. That you will not fall asleep tonight I take for granted. But whatever happens, and whatever you hear, do not leave your room until I call you."

After Holmes had obtained further information about the premises of Mr Archer's villa, the consultation was over, and the client took his leave. But from then on, my friend was like a different person: accessible, friendly, and humorous. The fish had entered the water; the bird had lifted its wing. The violin was put in its box, and we had dinner in a nice atmosphere.

The August evening was dark but mild when, shortly after nine o'clock, two dark figures cautiously, listening to every sound, strolled up to the eastern gable of Mr Archer's villa, concealed as best they could by the shrubbery of the yard. The dark figures were Sherlock Holmes and myself.

The living-room windows were easy to open - Holmes had, of course, informed himself of their position at Archer's - we swung ourselves in, closed them carefully behind us, and then, shoes in hand, made our way up the spiral staircase and were soon standing in the corridor. Holmes reconnoitred the terrain - his gifts include the sight of a lynx and the stride of a cat. "All is quiet," he whispered on returning from his reconnaissance, "in the kitchen, the servants are eating their supper, the front door is locked, and the electric light is off in the halls and stairways. We position ourselves here near the staircase; the perpetrator or perpetrators, for there may be two, must pass through here. But not a sound or a movement, Watson, until I command."

We stood silent and motionless, pressed tightly against the wall; everything around us was in the deepest darkness. At first, there were occasional rattles from the kitchen, but they soon ceased - early habits in this house. After that, everything was as dead; darkness and silence as in the grave prevailed.

The waiting time is always slow, but it creeps forward twice as slowly in a situation like ours. To pass the time, I went over the royal history of England, all the North Pole expeditions, and all the symptoms of disease known to pathology in my mind. However, my knees began to stiffen, imperceptibly bending my left leg. Imperceptibly? No, not at all! A silent "Shh!" told me that Holmes had heard and disapproved of my movement.

We heard the clock in the dining room strike ten, and it struck eleven. Nothing happened, nothing suspicious, nothing to suggest that a human being was approaching. My legs were now becoming as numb as an Indian fakir's, my arms were crawling like thousands of ants, and my eyelids wanted to fall shut. A nocturnal bug settled on my nose; it tickled unbearably. I lifted my finger and pricked it away; again, my friend's warning,

"Shh!" whispered in my ear like a ghostly whisper. Now, my patience began to fail. How long would we stand there like Nubian doormen in a harem? Would the culprit never come? I was just in the mood to take up a fight against him, despite his poisoned weapons. As my legs went numb, a dull hatred grew in my mind against the criminal as well as the representative of justice, against the detective as well as the culprit, against the Indian heritage and against my own stupidity that had brought me here, when I could have slept peacefully in my good bed. Why did I involve myself in an adventure that might bring me a stab in the body or a scratch from a poisoned weapon, but never an ounce of honour or profit? - Both always went to my friend and master. He was always the one; I was never anything but the zero, destined only to multiply his greatness.

While I was turning over these thoughts, the clock struck twelve. I couldn't stand it any longer. I was just about to say, "I'll give you..." when I was stopped by a sound, a faint but very distinct sound: the grinding of metal on metal. A key was being turned into a lock. Then there were slow, stealthy footsteps, first down the hall, then on the stairs.

At once, my joints' stiffness and my mind's irritation were gone. I silently apologised to my friend Holmes for my evil thoughts and admitted that he was never mistaken.

Now, the pawing steps were close upon us. Then a shrill cry cut through the silence of the night, and at the same moment, I heard Holmes' voice: "Up with the blind, Watson!"

The light of the lantern illuminated the scene before my eyes. Like a panther, my friend had thrown himself upon the unsuspecting criminal and wrapped his arms around him so that he stood there captive, unable to resist. In this vice, however, he was only a few seconds; I heard a clang of metal, and then the Hindu's wrists were adorned with an ornament glittering in the light: Holmes's safe, neat, patented handcuffs. Many times, I saw my friend put these on his victims, but I never could figure out how it was done. It seemed that Holmes had both his hands occupied elsewhere, but in a flash, before the criminal or anyone else realised what had happened, the bracelets were in place. You never knew which to admire more, Holmes' speed and certainty in his deductions or actions.

The battle was over - there had been hardly anyone; the victor wanted to claim his spoils.

"Light here, doctor, light on our Indian friend. Let's take a closer look at the poetic 'Labourer of the Night.'" In his victorious mood, my friend was happy to be a little humorous. "A bad labour and a bad merit tonight, eh, sahib? ... Ah, so young! Only the boy! The collector must have married late. Besides, you know, Watson, that Easterners are always more sprightly than sons of old England, and look much younger than they are. And he is hardly more tanned than an English boy after a sunny summer. His father was an Englishman, too, and dismay makes one pale. Lie still, sahib Ali or Isnu or whatever your name may be; your hands are safely tied, and you cannot escape. But now, Watson, we must reassure Mr Archer; I fear he is perishing with worry. Hey there, sir! Come on out! The danger is over; the bird is caught."

The bird had stood speechless with surprise with some vain attempts to tear off his shackles. Now, he finally got the sense to stammer out: "What do you want from me? Let me go! What harm have I done?" Because of his agitated state of mind, his voice was so indistinct and stammering that we could hardly make out the words. We paid little heed to his protests - the same ones that every criminal in his situation makes on his lips. Something else entirely occupied our attention.

Mr Archer cautiously opened his door but did not come out: "Is the danger really over?" he asked in a trembling voice. "Can the beast not murder me? Have you taken away his poisoned weapons, sir? I am so afraid of them."

"Stay where you are until I have searched him," replied Holmes, moving from words to action. In the meantime, my attention was drawn elsewhere. Down the hall, there were hurried footsteps. The electric light suddenly flared up in the staircase and corridor, and three women and a man, all in night clothes, rushed up the stairs; they were, of course, the house's servants.

One of the women was several steps ahead of the others.

"Mary, look out! What if there are thieves!" cried a warning voice from her companions. So it was Mary, the head housemaid, the accomplice in the plot against the master's life; she could be bolder and in more of a hurry than the others for this reason. Something of the spirit of Holmes came over me. Just as she reached the top of the stairs, and before she could give her accomplice any sign or message, I seized her arms with a firm grip - they were bare, round, and soft, by the way - and held her fast. She gave a cry, made some violent movements to free herself, and hurled the angry words in my face:

"Who are you? How dare you? Get your hands off me! Nasty man, you don't want to kiss me, do you? Can't you see that I'm a decent girl?"

But at the same time, I heard Holmes, half to himself, half to me, announce the results of the search he was making: "Wallet - of course - 3 shillings and pennies; matches, ordinary; folding knife, rough, large, much used, a simple weapon; ah! Corpus delicti! - Look here, Watson! A case, wickerwork of a foreign grass, something like what we encountered in the Andamanese - you remember the story of the sign of the four? If we open the case, we will see the poisoned weapons; trust it, Watson!"

Slowly and carefully, he opened the case. I leaned back slightly to make out its contents clearly; these were four Egyptian cigarettes, nothing else. Holmes's face lengthened; for the first time, I heard from his mouth the words: "What is this? I do not understand this."

Meanwhile, the trio had realised the situation downstairs and were chanting: "There's a thief in the house! And two policemen have caught him!" I had no time, however, to pay any attention to either the trio or Holmes' musings, for when my prey, Mary, saw my attention turned from her, she wrenched herself from my grasp with a sudden jerk, and with a well-directed blow to the chest sent me back three cubits against the wall, whereupon she assumed a victorious attitude of defence, ready to repel any attack, exclaiming, "Impertinent fellow, thief or policeman or whatever you may be, don't try to touch me! I am a decent English girl, and this is my house, that is, my master's. - And you, Will Sparrow," she directed this latter part of her indignation down the stairs, "what kind of a man are you to allow your fiancée to be molested without coming to her aid?"

It was not Will who answered; it came from another direction, from the prisoner. Hitherto turned away from the staircase and partially obscured by the pedestal of a statue; he now made a half-turn with the cry, "Mary!"

At the sound of her name, the girl took a few steps forward so that she could look into the prisoner's face. "Jim!" she shouted. "My God, it's Jim they've taken!"

Egged on by his fiancée's words and actions, Will Sparrow - the servant - plucked up his courage and came up, closely followed by the cook and other maids, and again, the three-part chorus rang out.

"Jim! It really is Jim! It certainly is not the young gentleman!" At the same time, Archer stuck his head out of the door: "What is it? Is there something the matter with my..." He did not finish the sentence, but stood as if pinned, with one hand on the lock, and his eyes as wide open and motionless as if he had been struck.

"What - means - this?" he finally stammered.

Holmes made a presenting hand gesture towards his prisoner. "Come out, Mr Archer! All clear, sir. Here we have the Hindoo, the culprit, the murderer."

"Has the young gentleman been murdered?" the servant asked angrily.

"Oh my God! Jim has killed!" screamed the second maid.

"Unhappy children! Why did he do that?" sobbed the cook.

"Nonsense!" Mary exclaimed. "Jim hasn't murdered any more than I have. He's a good boy. All this is just a fabrication of the police."

"Jim a murderer?" Archer said, now stepping out to us. "Impossible. Would my boy, my Jim, be a murderer?"

"Your boy?" Holmes and I asked simultaneously.

"Yes, indeed, my son Jim Perkins Archer."

"Of course, it's the young gentleman," confirmed four voices around us.

Surrounded by familiar and apparently sympathetic people, the prisoner plucked up courage: "What is this horrible business, Dad? What do these men want with me? Get me out of these - they're squeezing me -" he held up the handcuffs so that their shiny surface glistened in the light.

A general cry of surprise, which quickly turned into indignation and threatening mutterings. "Jim is in jail! Poor boy! Take the cloth off him, or else...!" Mary devoted a special tirade to my person: "It's that rough fellow's invention, I'm sure. If he'd had time, he'd have put me in chains, too."

At all this, I stood as stunned and perplexed as a five-year-old Eskimo boy would stand in the crowd on London Bridge. What could all this mean? My soul was filled with certain unpleasant forebodings; again, I wished I had been lying in my good bed at home that night instead of taking part in my friend's nocturnal excursion. I looked at Holmes, and even his features expressed anything but contentment. But the great thing about him was that he mastered every situation, even the most difficult.

With reverent calm and all the authority of a judge, he turned to his prisoner and asked, "Are you not a Hindu?"

"Hindu?" repeated the defendant. "Have you no eyes, sir, or are you mad?"

My friend did not mind the rudeness. As reverently as before, he turned to Archer and asked, "Is this your son?"

"Yes, of course, I told you."

"And you, my friends and witnesses present here, confirm this statement?"

Mr. Holmes's solemn tone and the officially legal form of the question made a deep impression on those to whom it was put; for a few moments, they seemed to ponder with themselves in the lively feeling of the weight of the answer, but then came a unanimous "yes."

"Then a mistake has been made," Holmes decided, taking from his pocket a small key and freeing Jim from the unpleasant bracelets. So superior and yet gentle was his whole demeanour in doing this, that not only did the threatening mutterings entirely cease, but all present, Jim included, looked up to my friend with the same feeling as one receives the honours of a king. He seemed to everybody to be the incarnation of justice, gentleness, and human kindness. But over my innocent head, on the other hand, were poured out the bowls of wrath; the glances which were directed towards me, no doubt, indicated that in me was seen the evil genius of the situation, the cause of the night's unrest, and Jim's offence; especially in Mary's glance, there was a whole centner of resentment and contempt.

For a minute, Holmes indulged in the enjoyment of the silent admiration bestowed upon him - for such, he was far from insensible - then he said: "The matter is closed for the night. Mr Archer, you may go to your rest and order the servants to do the same. And listen! Have you got a couple of beds for me and my friend for the night? I want to stay and do some research here tomorrow."

"Of course, I have rooms; a couple are always ready for guests. Mary, see to it that the corner room and the yellow chamber are put in order at once," ordered Archer.

Mary subjected us to a scrutinising glance; as far as Holmes was concerned it was apparently very satisfactory, but I was decidedly Mary's black sheep. "Is that going to stay too?" she asked with a significant nod towards me, and when the master only replied with an ungracious, "Do as I say!" she went away with a wilful toss of her otherwise rather pretty head. The other servants also withdrew.

When we were alone, Archer asked anxiously: "But the Hindu, the murderer? We haven't caught him, have we?"

"You may rest assured of his safety tonight, sir. Either something has prevented him from coming here, or his accomplice has suspected something and warned him. In any case, the behaviour just now is warning enough for him to cancel any business for the night. But there is a day tomorrow, too, Mr Archer. We did not reach the goal by the straightest route, but we will take a detour and reach it."

"In any case, you make me so happy that you are staying here, gentlemen. And what do you say? I have hardly tasted a morsel all day - the worry, of course, gentlemen - and I am ravenously hungry; probably you are the same; the journey here and your night work should have given you an appetite. Wouldn't a little cold meat and a drop of wine be a good thing after work, watch and worry?"

We were preceded by young Jim, who, now that the danger was over, proved to be a lively, cheeky and outspoken young man.

"Excellent, Dad! You sometimes have brilliant ideas in your old head. Supé at one o'clock! It's like we're London snobs. Really cool! I'm so hungry I'm going to run downstairs and ask Dora to organise a really nice party." He disappeared before Holmes and I could express our opinion, which was also superfluous, as it essentially coincided with young Jim's.

Half an hour later, four of us were sitting loudly in the dining room at Brightstone Park at a set table that did all the honour to the cook's or Jim's goodwill to uphold the house's reputation for hospitality.

We had drunk our first glass of wine when Archer turned to his son: "Jim, why did you come home last night, when you were supposed to stay in Rawnbury-hill until the day after tomorrow?"

"Bob Stanton," replied Jim, with his mouth full, "got a telegram late last night to fill in at half-back in the 'Youngest Team' football match on Saturday; young Landsford had got a sore knee, Bob had to travel on the bounce to train, and so I came over on the evening train. I didn't bother to telegraph to you because you would have been sitting up waiting, and I didn't want that. The little mile from the station, I thought I could walk, and my master key was in my pocket. But no one has said a word about the reason for the ruckus last night. You thought I was a thief, didn't you?"

"Much worse, Jim," said the father, "a murderer."

"A murderer? The police took me for a murderer? That was awesome! So, you've been talking about a Hindu; what Hindu?"

"My cousin - my father's nephew."

"Dad, do you have a cousin who is Hindu? This is getting funnier and funnier. What does he want here, since you brought the police?"

"Murder me for the sake of the inheritance, you know, Jim," Archer said grimly.

"Oh, my goodness! Dad, you're getting really interesting in your old age. This is like a detective story. Oh, I get it now! You were supposed to catch the doe, and you got me. That's funny! But who discovered that Hindu cousin? You never talked about him before, Dad."

"I knew nothing about him until Mr. Sherlock Holmes here," Archer pointed to my friend, "informed me about him."

"Who?" shouted Jim. "Sherlock Holmes!" He dropped his knife and fork on the table. "Are you Sherlock Holmes, the great detective?"

"That's my name, young Jim," said Holmes modestly.

"The one all the books are about?"

"That's right."

"He's sitting at the table with me!" Jim exclaimed, looking at the sky, or rather the ceiling. "He's got me in handcuffs! I never dreamed of such a thing! Imagine when Bob finds out! He'll be green with envy. And it's no good Landon Heart poking me in the nose with his uncle the Colonel and his adventures in the Boer War - now I can put him in his place. I'll be the class hero for a whole month. And you," Jim turned to me, "you must be Dr Watson?"

"That's right, sir."

"I knew it. I've got all your books; I don't know any that are that cool, not even the Indian books. Mr Holmes! Do you want to make me really happy?"

"Gladly, my young friend," replied Mr Holmes graciously.

"Give me the handcuffs as a present - as a memento, you know. I'll show them to the boys. They'll be amazed."

Holmes scowled. "Handcuffs are not toys for children."

But Jim did not give in so easily. "In a way, sir, I have a right to them; you have put them on me yourself. I am a free Englishman, sir; my house is my castle. Give them to me! It is the least redress you can give me."

I thought the boy was right, and, like Archer, favoured his request. Holmes reluctantly handed the neat, shiny objects to Jim, who received them almost with reverence, and occupied himself for a good while studying their mechanism. At the same time, we elders conversed on indifferent matters.

Jim, however, was the kind of person who might be diverted from a particular line of thought for the moment, but always returns to it.

"How did Mr Holmes know the Hindu existed, and how did he know that the Indian relative would come tonight and try to murder you, Dad?"

"Well, you see, my boy, I found a letter behind the stove yesterday afternoon; there it all was. Mary is the Hindu's accomplice."

"Mary," Jim said disdainfully. "Oh, Mary doesn't do that sort of thing. She's a good girl."

"Yes, Jim. I've fed a snake from my own bosom," said Mr Archer, whom the port had made a little emotional.

"I don't believe it. Dad, can I see the letter?"

"Jim, my son, I don't like it when the egg wants to teach the hen to lay. Mr Holmes has laid it all out so clearly that a blind man can see it. Remember, you're only a schoolboy, Jim. By the way, read it yourself. Here's the letter."

It was most interesting to watch the expression on young Jim's face as he smoothed out the crumpled paper on the table and looked at it. Never before or since have I seen a pair of boy's eyes so close to falling out of his head.

"Is this the letter from the Hindu?"

"Yes, of course," replied the father. "You can't read it properly, of course, but Mr Holmes..."

"Oh, my goodness! This was the coolest thing of all! It surpasses the books."

Jim's whole being shook with the most violent fit of laughter. He had to lean against the table to keep from falling off his chair. This unseemly expression of joy produced a dark cloud on the brow of my friend Holmes—he is strongly attached to the proper behaviour of young people. Even Archer, though a rather weak father, felt compelled to show his displeasure.

"You are behaving badly, sir! Is that the sort of behaviour you learn in Sir Edward's family?"

Jim tried to contain his mirth, but his speech was interrupted by constant fits of laughter. "Don't get mad,

Dad, but I can't help it - it's too crazy - if you knew, you'd..."

"Then tell me what you're laughing at, you ill-bred boy!" Archer made a threatening motion with his hand.

"Dad - it's so incredibly funny - that letter - I wrote it."

"You? You?" sounded in unison our three astonished voices.

"Yes, that's me."

"Hey, Jim? Did you want to murder your father? And with poisoned weapons?" The agitation and the port wine made Archer pathetic.

"Oh, you're so stupid," Jim retorted, somewhat disrespectfully. "I didn't want to murder you, or anyone else for that matter. After all, you're a real honourable old man, you know I think so, and I don't know anyone in the world who cares about me, except you."

"So why do you write such horrible letters, Jim?"

My friend Holmes felt that the circumstances required his personal intervention. "Mr Archer, you have left this matter in my hands: allow me to bring it to a conclusion. Let us proceed logically, and only so shall we reach the goal. Young Jim, did you write this letter?"

"Sure."

"When?"

"The day before yesterday."

"Under what circumstances?"

"Well, if you must know, during Latin class at school."

"Where did you get the paper?"

"I tore a page out of my dictionary."

"How do you explain that a piece of paper is missing?"

"Mr Ribbon, our other teacher, caught me writing instead of listening to his explanation of Livy. I was afraid he would come and read what I had written, so I tore up the sheet and threw one piece on the floor, but when I saw that he did not care to leave the desk, I put the other in my pocket."

"How did this remnant of the letter end up behind the stove?"

"Yesterday, when I was travelling to Rawnbury-hill, I was in a great hurry not to miss the train. Walking through the corridor, I felt the paper, pencil stub, and broken chess piece in my trouser pocket. I didn't want to take the rubbish with me to Rawnbury-hill, so I threw it behind the stove. Maybe the other stuff is still there."

"Your testimony, young Jim, has the stamp of truth, and you possess, sir - let me congratulate you on it - a not inconsiderable logical acumen. But one more thing: for what purpose did you write that letter?"

Jim blushed. "Is it necessary for me to tell you?"

"Absolutely. Justice requires complete clarity in all details."

"Very well then. You see, gentlemen, as Dad likes to say, we boys in the fifth form have a literary club. We have meetings every Thursday night, when we read what we've written. Some of them come up with poems and stuff like that; others write essays on Ruskin or on 'the English woman as wife and mother' - it's stupid, and most of it's stolen from books and newspapers, of course, but you can believe, sir, that they strut like peacocks about it. But Bob Stanton and I agreed to outshine them all, and Bob said to me: 'We're going to write a detective story, the sort of thing Watson writes about Sherlock Holmes, and we'll borrow a bit from those books that you, Jim, know almost by heart. The boys will be amazed and envious. – So, Bob said, and we were off to work: it's about a Kaffir chief's revenge on a Boer farmer and an English detective's discovery of the crime. We had just reached the third chapter, in which the Kaffir, with the help of a Bushman who serves in the Boer's house, is going to carry out his revenge, and I had been given the task of writing a letter about this from the Kaffir to the Bushman. During the lesson, I had a good idea for it, which I wanted to write down before it was forgotten."

"Well, young Jim, your explanation is satisfactory. But why did you write that about the poplars and the third door? It fits this place, your father's farm, but not a Boer's home. There are no poplars there."

"It doesn't exist? I didn't realise that. When we were going to describe the Boer's home in the first chapter, Bob wanted us to use Rawnbury-hill as a model, but it's a castle, and the Boers don't live in castles, so we decided to have the Boer live on a farm like this, with poplars and everything."

During the interrogation, Jim's desire to laugh had completely disappeared. I almost suspect that in the face of my friend's judgemental dignity and inquisitorial approach, he felt like an accused, almost a criminal. The rest of us, Archer and I, had listened with amazement and interest.

At the end of the hearing, Mr Holmes sat for a moment in silent contemplation, after which he spoke.

"Mr Archer! My mission here is complete, and tomorrow morning my friend and I will return to London. But let me congratulate you. You may, in the future, live in peace without fear of the Indian cousin. He is dead; indeed, more than that, he never existed."

"Mr Holmes, what do you say? Is it all a mistake? Have we been running for nothing, sir?"

With unwavering dignity, my friend replied:

"Mr Archer! You gave me a letter. It contained threats of criminal revenge. What did I promise you? To arrest the letter writer and bring him before you as a prisoner. What have I done? Who wrote the letter? Young Jim. And did he not stand before you an hour ago with his wrists cuffed? As far as I can see, I have fulfilled my undertaking and thrown light on the whole affair."

"Oh, you're right, sir," Mr Archer admitted, "you're always right."

"I am never wrong," Mr Holmes stated.

"This was the coolest detective story I ever dreamed of," Jim exclaimed. "And to think it's true, and I lived it myself!"

The following morning, my friend Sherlock Holmes and I were on the train to London. Holmes was mostly occupied with the Times, but suddenly, he said:

"Watson, you don't have to write a book about this."
And I haven't done that either.

3. The Princess of Bandalore

I HAD sent the issues of the Stockholms Dagblad to Dr Watson, in which I had reported our conversations about his friend Sherlock Holmes. As I had heard that he was still in the country, while I had returned to London, I was very pleasantly surprised when one day I saw him come into my room.

"Thank you for the reports," he said kindly. "They are very good, that is, I suppose they are. As you know, no writer reads what others have written, and besides, I don't speak Swedish. But I'm sure the reviews are good - I fully agree with the principle of our modern newspaper criticism: you don't judge the work but the author. I like you, Stig, therefore what you write is good. But I am unhappy with one passage in your letter, which is a cruel misinterpretation of my friend Holmes."

I was very surprised. I thought I had only said flattering things about the doctor's famous friend, and I said it.

"You have misinterpreted him, as has the whole world. You write: 'It is regrettable that so richly endowed a spirit should lack an essential trait in a male character: the sense of feminine charm'. Who said it was so?"

The doctor was almost angry. I apologised as best I could. "You never touched on that side of him in your books, not even with a hint."

The doctor lowered his head guiltily. "You are right: I have unintentionally been the cause of the world's wrong judgement. Well, Stig, if you have the time and the inclination, I would like to make amends for my error, at least to you."

I had both time and desire in abundance. We lit our cigars, and the doctor sat down comfortably in my armchair and began to talk.

One day, I received the following message from Sherlock Holmes: "Napoleon always had his historian with him; his name was Bourienne. You are my Bourienne. Make yourself free and visit me. Great things are happening. Holmes."

I was taking time off; my internship never got in the way of that - the public thinks that anyone who writes good books must write bad recipes - and my wife had travelled to visit acquaintances - we had been married for two years, and she now visited her acquaintances very often.

So a couple of hours later, I was sitting in my usual place in the Holmes reception room, boredly leafing through a magazine, with my friend opposite me. You recognise the situation from my books; it is always the same. Holmes was rubbing out strange notes from his violin, but suddenly interrupted his playing: "Watson, what kind of pen do you use when you write?"

I looked up in surprise - in the face of Sherlock Holmes, surprise is my permanent state.

"Of course, steel pen," I replied.

"Of course. But now, get yourself a pen of gold. It was used to sign the peace treaties of Prague and Frankfurt, and you are going to write a more important document than these ambiguous agreements. I am about to win a victory comparable to Nelson's at Trafalgar. My vigour and sagacity are at their height."

My whole person formed a living question mark. Holmes smiled.

"You know nothing, the world knows nothing, the six million creeping creatures we call London know nothing. I alone know and act, organising my armies for a giant battle. I lead them unseen through obscure hollow ways until they irresistibly break forth and crush the enemy into atoms. What happens big, happens quietly. But in eight days' time, England and Europe will be astonished. Listen, Doctor, you know Moriarty?"

"The professor? Yes, of course."

"You know he is the greatest villain on earth, a freak, a scourge of humanity; in his hand, he holds the threads of every atrocity committed in recent years, not only in England but on the Continent. Those nuts at Scotland Yard know it, but dare not point a finger at him; he laughs at them. There is only one man he fears, and that is me, Sherlock Holmes. Only to one living man has nature given greater gifts than to Moriarty. He has the brain of a genius and the finesse of a lord, he has enormous wealth at his disposal, and every country is swarming with his agents. He could have been a Newton or a Chamberlain, but he loves crime for crime's sake. That is why he will hang from the gallows, and I will be the one to take him there."

My friend paused, then continued:

"He and I are fighting a life-and-death struggle; in a few days, the decisive battle will be fought. He is a fish around which I have drawn my net; anxiously, he swims round to find an exit, but constantly bumps his head against the net. In the safe in my bedroom, I have papers that are the noose around his neck. Watson, do you realise now why you must write in gold pencil?"

I understood, but had nothing to answer; I felt only my smallness before this great man; he was Napoleon, I only Bourienne. No answer was needed, nor did my friend expect one. I was only the rock wall against which he shouted to hear the echo of his words returned to his ears. Holmes brought the violin to his chin, and with the full-toned sound of a full orchestra, he let out of the strings "Napoleon's March across the Alps" as a song of triumph.

In the middle of the music, the door opened, and a visitor entered. His appearance suggested a gentleman, even a man of the upper classes. Displeased at being disturbed, my friend glanced quickly at the intruder, and I thought I heard a false note, an A instead of an Ass, cut into the harmony. Perhaps it was a mistake, for Holmes continued to play unperturbed until he finished the rehearsal.

"Ah, you play 'Napoleon's March across the Alps,' Mr Holmes, and with real bravura," said the strange gentleman. "My belief is that Napoleon never used that march up in the Alpine passes; he was a man of genius who knew that the Alps have treacherous precipices and chasms, and that one should not play victory marches until the battle is won."

My friend smiled as he put down his violin. "Napoleon played the march when he reached the last slope of the Alps and knew he had Italy in his hands. But let me introduce you to my friend Dr Watson - Professor Moriarty."

I almost fell backwards. Moriarty here! The boa constrictor in the lion's den! The professor, however, pretended not to notice my astonishment.

"Who doesn't know Mr Holmes, the famous historian?" he said politely, after which he turned to my friend: "I come unexpectedly, but not untimely I hope?"

His manner was endearingly polite. I am pleased to say that my friend was no worse in this respect.

"By all means, Professor, no excuses! Your arrival is not at all untimely. I can tell you that I half expected a visit from you one of these days. Please be seated!"

Holmes pushed a chair forward. The guest glanced round quickly before sitting down. "I am alone, and the gentlemen are two, but I have no reason not to accept Mr Holmes' kind offer. You need not look at the table drawer where you keep your revolver, Doctor. I am quite unarmed; Mr Holmes knows that."

My friend nodded in agreement. As usual, my lot was to sit in amazement. The professor turned to me:

"You see, Doctor, Mr Holmes has his good reasons for not yet allowing any violent clash between us. He has not yet finished all his preparations; he knows that a blow now would be a blow in the air. Your friend is one of the wisest people alive. But what he may not know is that if I am not free and clear in Baker Street 35 minutes after this, No. 221B in the said street, that is to say, this very house, will be immediately blown up with a bang, and Mr Holmes wants to avoid that, if not for his own sake, for he is a brave man, then for the sake of some papers which he keeps in his bedroom safe."

I have experienced the horrors of the Afghan war, but I still blanched at the prospect of sitting directly over a booby-trapped mine. However, the professor kindly reassured me.

"No immediate danger, doctor! The disaster only occurs under certain conditions. The whole thing is limited to a few kilos of dynamite, buried in the foundations of the house, and a fine electric wire running to a house nearby, where there is a button to press. If no one touches the button, you will be as safe as the Lord Chancellor on his woollen sack."

In spite of these reassurances, my eyes still anxiously sought my friend Holmes. He sat outwardly unmoved, but from the movement of his shoulders, I noticed that he was shaken by an inward laugh.

"You are always prescient, Professor," he said politely. "I know the wire is there, and I suppose you are right about the button too. But how do you know the dynamite is there?"

"I've seen it put there myself," said the ever-benevolent professor.

"Last Thursday night, at 1.35 am," Holmes added. "Tom Whistley buried the package in the cellar and hid the wire in Mrs Somrith's, my housekeeper's, rubbish. But do you know who made the dynamite?"

"Certainly not. You make me curious, sir."

"The manufacturer is the one who now has the honour of talking to you. You can treat that dynamite with a sledge hammer or throw it into a red-hot blast furnace without risk of explosion."

My friend savoured his triumph for a second, after which he continued in a benevolently admonitory tone:

"You should not have trusted Tom, sir. That was stupid. He's been in my service for a fortnight."

"Tom!" Moriarty exclaimed. "Impossible!"

"Nothing is impossible, sir. Besides, the matter is not a magic trick. I knew that Tom had a sweetheart in Battersea, a waitress in a third-class inn; you did not, and therefore I could take him from you. The woman and the love, sir, were the strings I pulled, and so he had to dance to my tune. Women, sir, are the source of all the foolishness in the world; avoid them like the plague, except when you need them as strings to pull. Don't be angry with poor Tom, it's no use. He is already far beyond your reach."

For a few seconds, the professor had lost his good-natured politeness, but only for a few seconds. He nodded in agreement and said: "Excellent, Mr Holmes, almost genius! If I were French, I would applaud. But your polite sincerity demands a response. Look here, gentlemen, this miniature box. If I press this little spring, a sweetish odour will immediately spread through the room. Beware of it! If you breathe it in for just two seconds, within 30, you'll be as stone dead as old King Arthur in his sarcophagus. It is ba-ha-tai poison; you, Mr Holmes, know it."

"What would happen to you?" my friend asked.

"Don't worry about me. I took half a gram of Oxygeton sulphuris melanopyrati as I was going up the stairs just now, and that, as you know, is an infallible antidote."

"And I, too, have taken it three times today, as I have done every day since I learnt that you had the poison in your possession. So it is only poor Watson who runs the risk." Holmes' laughter was almost audible, and he was apparently in a downright jovial mood. Well, he could laugh, but I certainly had no reason to. Even Moriarty seemed to find the situation amusing.

"You are a master, Mr Holmes, even my master, I admit it," he said.

My friend was far from insensitive to the compliments of such an authority; his face assumed an expression that did not often appear there: that of modest complacency, and he bowed slightly.

Suddenly the professor changed his tune: "But, Mr Holmes, we look like children when we play with these toys. What is the use of these ridiculous precautions? You can't arrest me; such a rash step would upset all your great plans. So we can sit down quietly and discuss, and indeed I have come here to open a discussion with you."

"Here you go."

"You are a wise man, sir, and I am no fool either, but fate has brought us into opposite camps and made us adversaries; in the end, it has come between us to a fight to the death. Who will prevail? No one knows, we only know that one of us must perish, and that in any case, the world will suffer a great loss, it will lose one of its most gifted minds. Is this a situation worthy of two rational men?"

"Where are you going, sir?"

"Let us make peace. May we part ways! I will leave the field here in England free for you and seek another sphere of activity."

"In your previous industry?"

"Who knows? We don't have the gift of prophecy now, Mr Holmes. Maybe, maybe not... This is also outside the scope of our negotiations. The question is simply this: If you will let me leave England unmolested, I promise you that I will not set foot on its soil again, nor will I carry on any business on this side of the Channel."

Holmes thought for a minute, but no longer.

"No, I don't want that, Moriarty. I do not want it. I can sympathise with a wretched person who has broken the law in a moment of passion or distress, but you, you are the leader of the worst band of thieves and murderers that has defiled the soil of England for three centuries; you have the devil in your heart, and therefore I will not stop until I see you dangling from the gallows..."

"Or lying somewhere like a corpse," the professor added.

"Exactly," my friend replied coldly. "You have fully understood the situation."

The professor stood up and lightly stroked his shiny hat with his coat sleeve. "So you reject my offer. Well, I've done what I could, you'll have to bear the consequences. Au revoir, Mr Holmes, goodbye, Doctor!"

He walked calmly and carefree towards the door, my friend made no attempt to stop him. He remained in his armchair, lost in thought. "What a man!" I heard him murmur in an admiring tone. "What a pity the world has no room for us both, him and me!"

*

SCARCELY five minutes later a carriage stopped outside our gate, and we heard the rustle of silk outside our door. The door opened, waves of perfumed air rushed towards us, and a lady in the most discreetly fashionable attire stood before us. She might have been about 40 years of age, and everything in her posture, manner, and language testified to the educated lady, a real lady, with youth and charm well preserved for her age.

"Mr Holmes, I presume?" She said, turning to me.

"I'm Mr Holmes," my friend replied. "This is Dr Watson. All England knows us, but you are excused, for you are a stranger in London."

The lady looked at my friend in wonder. "How on earth do you know that? How do you know me?"

"I do not know you at all, but I see that you have come to England - let us say two months ago. I see in you four characteristics that cannot deceive."

"Oh, Mr Holmes! It is true, then, what I have read of your marvellous acumen? It is precisely to employ it that I have taken the liberty of calling upon you."

"I'm sorry, but my time is taken up with other, bigger tasks. I cannot be of service to you," my friend said sternly. "Turn to Scotland Yard!"

"There? To the idiots there? No way."

My friend's face brightened. "My lady, you have a rare quality in women: you have judgement."

"Oh, Mr Holmes, I am flattered to hear you say that. I don't suppose you think very highly of the woman."

"No great man does that. Woman has no logic, no thinking power, no brain. She is a phonograph that only repeats what men have told her."

"Perhaps you do the woman an injustice, Mr Holmes. But to you, it is natural to think so. To one who stands on the top of the dome of St Paul's Cathedral, the people crawling in the streets must seem like little pygmies."

My friend smiled gently and beautifully. "Not badly said, my lady. You have spoken a profound truth."

"Mr Holmes, you are very kind, too kind and good to send a poor inferior woman away without help and comfort."

To my surprise, my friend replied: "Please sit down, my lady, and tell me the reason for your visit. I will see if I can do anything for you. But be as brief as possible."

"Oh, how amiable you are, Mr Holmes!" The lady sat down, pushed back her white feather boa and began:

"My name is Whalters, Lydia Whalters, widow of Major John Whalters of the Third Bengal Mountain

Artillery. On the death of my beloved John" - she brought her batiste handkerchief to her eyes, causing a cloud of perfume to float across the room - "I returned to England, where I arrived seven weeks ago with my protégé Dar Mila."

"Who?" Holmes interrupted. "Dar Mila? Male or female?"

"A young girl of 19 years."

"A girl! Leave aside all trivialities."

"Dar Mila is not an insignificant person. She is a princess."

"Ah, a princess! That changes things. You are very interesting, my lady. Please continue."

"Her father was Dar Singh, the Prince of Bandalore - perhaps you don't know Bandalore?"

"I know everything, my lady. Bandalore is in India."

"Oh, Mr Holmes, you are right. You know all about it. Then you know that Bandalore is a small kingdom, of only six or seven million people, but nevertheless, the prince is one of the richest rulers in India. That is thanks to the diamond mines, you see. Dar Singh was a friend of my husband's - oh, how many glorious days we spent in the Prince's garden castle at Rivapuptra, a veritable fairytale castle, Mr Holmes! So I don't want to say anything derogatory about Dar Singh, but I feel there is nothing to hide from you. Well, Dar Singh was an Indian ruler, that is to say, a little too much of a despot and a little too capricious; he treated the lives and property of his subjects rather lightly. The result was a revolution in which Dar Singh lost his crown and his life, and his nephew, Sandar Singh, the author of the event, took the throne. Fortunately, Dar Mila was rescued by a faithful servant and escaped to us, to John and me. She was only 15 at the time, and had been forced to flee as she walked and stood. A small bundle of clothes and a box of diamonds worth one or two million was all she could take with her.

She stayed with us until poor John died - he was so fond of plum pudding with hot sauce, and the plum pudding killed him. I then returned to England, and Dar Mila came with me.

In London, surprising news awaited us from Bandalore. Dar Singh had not exactly been what you call the father of his people, but with Sandar Singh, they had risen from the ashes of the fire. The outraged people had also ousted Sandar and proclaimed Dar Mila as their ruler. As soon as the negotiations with the British Government were concluded, Dar Mila would travel to Bandalore, and I would of course, follow her.

You will think, Mr Holmes, that I have been far too long-winded, but remember that I am only a woman! You would, of course, have put it all in five words."

My friend nodded in agreement. "Please continue."

"I now come to the matter for which I sought you out. Oh, Mr Holmes! It is all so strange and frightfully mysterious. As you know - though you don't - Dar Mila has her bedroom inside mine; there is no entrance to it except through my bedchamber. One morning I am lying awake thinking of poor John - I do that most nights, sir - when I hear Dar Mila scream. I rush in to see her, and she is sitting upright in bed, holding between her fingers a strange gem. She had found it on her bedside table when she woke up, but it had not been there when she went to bed, and none of the servants had set foot in the room during the night, as you see, Mr Holmes. But soon something even more terrible was to happen. One morning, a few days later, she found in the same place a sharply sharpened dagger, and this morning a small wooden box containing five small bullets. Oh, Mr Holmes, you who know everything, tell me what this means!"

Cold and unconcerned as usual, my friend had listened to the lady's story, but the dark shadow that settled over his features showed that he took the matter seriously.

"Let me see the objects," he said briefly.

"Oh, Mr Holmes, can you believe I would bring such terrible things? Dar Mila has them lying on a shelf in her sitting room."

"Then how do you expect me to express myself?" my friend said almost angrily, but quickly softened his tone. "But you are a woman. In some cases, you have judgement, but you are still a woman."

"Oh, Mr Holmes, I am so sorry that I am so stupid and thoughtless, but as you say, I am only a woman. You won't leave me in my helplessness?" Mrs Whalters almost wept with humiliation and anguish.

I always admire my friend, but seldom has he seemed so magnanimous as at this moment, when he replied: "My lady, if I were a Frenchman, I should answer: madame, I am infinitely sorry, only matters of the utmost importance prevent me from serving you, but I am an Englishman, and I feel my duty to a princely person, even if her skin is coloured. I know that blue blood is of a different quality from ordinary red. It shall be my honour to devote my service to Her Royal Highness, Dar Mila. My lady, your address?"

"Cupperhill, Strutton Lane."

"Can you take us in your carriage?"

"With pleasure. Oh, Mr Holmes, how kind you are!"

Two minutes later, we were in the carriage, which rolled away to Mrs Whalter's home. During the journey, the said amiable lady used the time to give us some important information. "Mr Holmes, Dr Watson, you must not interfere with poor Mila's little idiosyncrasies, promise me! Remember that she grew up in an Indian harem as the daughter of an autocrat, used to commanding hundreds of servants. You must not be surprised if she has a firm will and wants no obstacles to her desires. But there is something even stranger about her. Can you believe it, that she abhors all men? She regards them as narrow, low-minded, cunning, selfish natures, creeps - she judges, of course, by the types she saw in Bandalore. When she was in Simla with me and Blessed John, she was naturally surrounded by a whole host of admirers, but she was cold to everybody, cold as the Himalayan snow. 'Dear children,' I used to say to her, 'remember that Lord Chatters belongs to one of the most noble families in England, and that Captain Billonsbury is the son of a marquis! You should have seen the look on her face when she replied: 'What business is it of mine - yes, she really used that expression - what business is it of mine if the man to whom I would give myself and my crown is a street sweeper or a prince? I shall never marry but to him whom I love, and he shall be a superior spirit, superior in sagacity, superior in courage; that is all he need be."

This information did not, of course, diminish our interest in the Princess; the opinions of a princely person may seem strange to us, but they always attract our attention, and usually our favour.

*

WE arrived at Cupperhill, a rather modest building surrounded by a small park. After Mrs Whalters had announced our arrival, we were ushered into Her Ladyship's drawing room.

It was, of course, decorated in a sort of Oriental style, filled with colourful draperies, carpets, and cushions; otherwise, the furniture was very sparse: a couple of low tables, a soft divan, a few stools, some trinkets on a shelf, including a hideous Buddha statue made of simple clay. Although it was not yet dusk, the curtains were drawn, and a pendant lamp cast a subdued, rose-coloured glow over the room; the oil was apparently perfumed and gave off a strong, almost intoxicating fragrance. The whole scene was not calculated to give too high an idea of either the wealth or the taste of the princess, but Oriental eyes see differently from European ones, and

    FRANS OSKAR WÅGMAN

we were not in the fairy-tale castle of Rivapura, but in a house rented by the month on Strutton lane.

Besides, who cares whether the setting is gold or copper, when the eye is dazzled by the sparkling diamond? I once wrote in one of my books: "In my intercourse with women of several nations on three continents, I have never seen a more delightful creature." The words then applied to Miss Morstan, later Mrs Watson. In the interests of truth, I must correct them in Her Ladyship Dar Mila's favour. There she was, at our entrance, stretched out on the divan, leaning on her left elbow, presenting the picture of perfect Eastern beauty. Fine-limbed, with ideal harmony in every line of the body, in every movement, with facial features like an Eastern Venus, skin like the ripe peach with a light shade of brown, eyes, almond-shaped, black as night, dreamy, but with fire in the depths - ah, Stig, Titian, Raphael, Murillo have not even dreamed of anything more ravishing. And how well her attire suited this exotic beauty: a yellow silk gown held together at the waist by a red belt, more revealing than concealing the perfection of her figure, her bare arms up to the shoulder were adorned with golden bracelets, her similarly bare feet - Cinderella would have blanched with envy - were tucked into silver embroidered slippers. Unbidden I was reminded of the expression quoted above from my book, and I felt it a matter of conscience to correct it, especially on recalling Mrs Watson's pointed, now somewhat reddish nose and her far from beaked shoe size.

Mrs Whalters introduced: "Mr Holmes, Dr Watson."

The Princess responded with only a slight bow of the head, but what a background of both grace and majesty in this simple movement!

As usual, Holmes had an eye only for honour, not for beauty, and a mind only for his mission. "Your Highness," he said, with a deep bow, but in his business-like manner, "be so good as to show me the objects which have so strangely come into your possession."

"Mrs Whalters can do it," replied the Princess, with a foreign accent but in a voice as sweet as the evening wind in the cypresses at the Fountain of Tears in Coimbra. Mrs Whalters completed the task, and my friend began her examination of the objects.

"This stone," he said, "is a chrysoprase of not very high value, which is further diminished by the multicoloured ring in its centre. Part of the setting is still there; the stone has been violently broken away from its place."

"From my father's crown," Dar Mila said.

"Ah, from a royal crown! Tell me all you know about this stone!" In his eagerness, my friend completely forgot his reverence for the royal blood. Dar Mila sent him a surprised look, but said:

"The stone was the tip of a lamidji flower that adorned the crown; it was the most precious jewel of the treasure, worth a thousand times its weight in gold, precisely because of the multicoloured ring. This ring makes the stone a sacred jewel, the 'Eye of Indra', an amulet that protects its wearer from all evil. The stone was stolen three nights before my father lost his crown and life."

"Watson," exclaimed my friend, "here is material for your gold pencil." He then brought up the next item for examination.

"Oriental dagger, simple silver handle, the blade double-edged, running into a sharp point, probably poisoned; gold inlay along the blade in the form of a narrow leaf tendril, interrupted on one side by three newly engraved circles. What do you know about this dagger, Princess?"

"Nothing."

"You haven't seen it before, for example in Bandalore?"

"Never."

Holmes took the third object in his hand.

"Round, a small box of sandalwood - Indian work; inside five balls resembling an apothecary's pills, black, each with an almost invisible white spot; the smell peculiar, nauseating, recognisable among a thousand others. The pellets are the seeds of Evonistas mortifera, a shrub from the mountains of Dean. Its name mortifera, the deadly, is given because every creature that breathes its vapour for ten minutes is doomed to certain death."

"Oh, Mr Holmes, throw those dreadful balls out of the window!" Mrs Whalters shouted in horror.

"Don't worry!" my friend reassured her. "The bullets are completely harmless; only the leaf-bearing bush can kill. The seeds only have a symbolic meaning. Do you know this meaning, your honour?"

"Not at all."

"Well, we'll get to that later. Tell us how you found these things."

"Mrs Whalters has told you. When I woke up in the morning, they were on my bedside table, which had been empty in the evening."

"And no-one had been in your room during the night?"

If looks could kill, my friend would never again have exercised his marvellous powers on this sinful earth. At the flash of Dar Mila's beautiful eyes, even Holmes recoiled, he who did not shrink from the daggers and revolvers of murderers. Never have I seen him so impressed and embarrassed. "I apologise; I meant no offence," he stammered. "With Your Highness's permission, I will now begin some investigations of the premises" - and as if to escape the displeasure of the beautiful despot, he immediately set to work.

I don't need to describe these investigations; I've done it hundreds of times in my books, and I'm sick of it. They are always the same: there is snooping and looking with or without a magnifying glass, smelling and tasting everything, climbing trees, roofs and walls, gathering dust and cigar ash, measuring footprints, knocking on walls, whistling and wondering, asking the servants questions, making sudden remarks of incomprehensible content to anyone in the neighbourhood. Every educated person knows this by heart; the police officers in Paris and Trosa imitate it. I can skip it.

The examinations took more than a couple of hours. For me, they might have lasted a century, for I had the honour and pleasure of joining the ladies for refreshments in the Princess's drawing-room during a very pleasant conversation about the weather, the theatres, the football matches, and the recent mining accident, a truly educated conversation. As befits Her Highness, she was somewhat taciturn and princely dignified; Mrs Whalters, on the other hand, very entertaining and amiable.

Eventually, Sherlock Holmes joined us, but declined all refreshments.

"First, the results of my work," he said, sat down and began his presentation.

"I have hardly ever come across a darker case; everything deviates from the usual patterns. You, Mrs Whalters, who read the Doctor's books, will know that criminals are fond of choosing places for their deeds where the dust is in heaps, or the ground is marshy, or consists of soft garden soil, as if they wanted to leave their footprints as calling cards. Usually, they also have some peculiarity that makes them recognisable: a wooden leg that leaves round marks wherever they go, the foot of a savage, so unlike that of civilised people, a severed finger missing from the bloody handprints they leave on walls and doors. Not infrequently, after the deed is done, they sit down in an armchair to smoke their cigar, and the ashes they leave behind reveal their height, thickness, facial features and skin colour, level of education, habits and social status. But there is not a trace of any of this here; there is nothing at all."

"Oh, Mr Holmes, are we still as helpless as ever?"
Mrs Whalters exclaimed.

My friend smiled - it was Napoleon's smile at the
'prince's gathering' in Erfurt.

"Others would be at a loss, but I never am. For me,
there can be no riddles. I have had six solutions; one of
them is complete, it covers all circumstances. Listen to
me. The servants are outside the case. A red hair in the
pantry window - there last night at 11 o'clock - aroused
my suspicions for a moment, but it only meant a couple
of slices of mutton, a mug of beer and a dozen kisses -
the cook is a devoted admirer of the local police officer.
You have a good way with servants, Mrs Whalters. You
change them every fortnight."

"Or every eight days," the lady said.

"Very wise. In such things, women have a fine instinct.
That way you will always have attentive, diligent and
humble servants - they always are in the first week. I
repeat once more: you are a lady of judgement."

"Oh, Mr Holmes, you almost make me proud!"

My friend continued:

"The first question is: how did the objects get
into Her Honour's bedroom? I have examined all the
rooms; there is no crack in the ceiling, walls, walls or
floor, only one entrance, namely from the room where
Mrs Whalters watches over her beloved husband's
memory through the night. The objects must have
come in through the window. But how? The external
circumstances show us that. A rainwater drainage pipe
runs from the roof of the building to the ground right

next to Her Ladyship's window. Still, the stranger who brought the diamond, the dagger and the bullets has not been able to use the lower part of the pipe, which is completely rusted through and would not support even a child. Instead, he has climbed up the water pipe at the gable to the cornice above the third floor, balanced himself on it to the upper part of the downpipe, which is newly repaired, and on this, he has reached the window, which he has opened noiselessly - I can show you an instrument designed for this purpose, one of the finest electrotechnical inventions of the present day. Ladies, you wonder why you did not wake up when he entered the room, but you do use perfume diffusers to spread a nice scent? Well, others can use the same means to fill a room with anaesthetic vapours; you notice nothing, you fall asleep and sleep for three, five, or twenty hours, unaware of everything.

Who was the intruding stranger? No man in all England except the "snake man" of Lipton's circus and one other person whom I will not name - I hate self-praise, ladies - has sufficient courage, agility and presence of mind to balance on the cornice. But an Eastern man can; he is used to that. The stranger was an Eastern man, let us say a Hindu.

Did he come as a friend or foe? The latter would have plunged the dagger into Her Highness's breast, not left it on her bedside table. So, we can safely say that he came as a friend. For what purpose? Obviously to convey a message to Her Highness. But why in this secretive way with signs, not with clear, open words? There is not a shadow of a doubt as to the reason: implicated in a criminal plot by circumstances we cannot investigate, the stranger was bound to silence by one of those terrible Indian oaths which no Hindu dares to break. But if he dared not speak, he could act instead. Unconsciously, he was imitating Mrs Rebus, the woman who gave the riddles their name.

So, what was the content of his riddles? The meaning was so clear that a child could find it. A precious stone, cut out of your father's crown, was left to you, Princess; thus, you were notified of your investiture as heir to the throne. The dagger, the tool of the secret assassins, means that your life is threatened by fanatical enemies - note that the dagger was double-edged! - The rings on the blade indicate that the assassins are three; the oriental style of the weapon and the oriental style of the weapon show that they are Hindus, probably your cousin Sandar Singh's henchmen. The five bullets announce that the fifth day is now set for the fulfilment of the deed, and that at the very first dawn - the little white dot on the night-black seeds expresses the moment as clearly as words could. There you have it, ladies, the gist of the matter. I have 135 other details which are of importance to me, but with which I do not wish to trouble Her Highness."

My friend had finished his talk. Mrs Whalters sat as a picture of speechless dismay. I had experienced too many shocking and surprising events in the company of my friend Mr Holmes to feel any real fear, so I could observe with calmness the effect my friend's words had on Dar Mila. At first, she had shown an Oriental indifference, but gradually, her interest was aroused; it grew stronger and stronger, and soon I saw her bosom rise in ever quickening waves; her eyes took on a strange glow, and were kept fixed on my friend, as if she were afraid of missing a single word of his.

Holmes had fallen silent, there was a short pause: then something strange happened. Holmes said:

"Now, a drop of wine and water would suit me. Doctor, will you serve?"

Naturally, I was willing and reached for the decanter, but pulled it back as if stung by a snake. I was met by a look from Dar Mila's eye, sharp and piercing as a sword. Without a word, with the dignity of an empress and the grace of a fairy, she rose from the divan, walked to the serving table, filled a glass, touched its rim with her lips, and, kneeling, handed it to Sherlock Holmes.

We all sat in amazement.

"Your Royal Highness!" was all my friend could stammer. Mrs Whalters forgot her dismay for her astonishment: "Dar Mila! What are you doing?" she exclaimed, clasping her hands together.

Dar Mila remained in her kneeling position with her glass raised towards my friend.

"I salute a man; I bow the knee to superiority," she said calmly, and turning to Holmes, she continued: "Drink! And from the spot on the glass where a girl's pure lips have rested, Lakshmi, goddess of love and beauty, wife of the ever-worshipped Vishnu, make your heart as rich in warmth as your head is rich in wisdom and your soul in courage. Then you are the perfect one."

Holmes had experienced many strange events in his varied life, but never anything like this. A princess, and one of the most beautiful creatures on earth at that, was kneeling before him with an expression on her face such as Psyche must have had when she first fell into Cupid's arms, with a look as radiant as if Sirius, the Pleiades, the Southern Cross, and all the constellations of heaven had gathered their splendour therein.

The glass trembled in my friend's hand, spilling some of its contents; his pale cheeks flushed, and his eyes sought Mrs Whalters and me with an almost helplessly pleading hesitation. Then they fastened again on the lovely creature at his feet, and suddenly he raised the glass to the light to see the mark of Dar Mila's lips, and drained the drink. Proud as a goddess and with a radiant brow, the princess rose and returned to her place on the divan.

There was a long and deep silence. What could we say? We were all caught up in strange thoughts and feelings. Of course, it was Mrs Whalters who first regained her composure and spoke up - she was a woman.

"Oh, Mr Holmes! You have shown us what a terrible danger we are in. What are we to do? There is only one piece of advice: tonight, we pack our bags and go to Paris, Naples, Algiers, wherever, as long as we get away from this awful London."

Thus brought into his own domain, Holmes immediately regained his composure and determination.

"No, Mrs Whalters, you shall not. Her Highness's enemies would follow in her wake with fresh attacks, and I would not be there to ward them off. There shall not a hair of her noble head be touched, I swear it. I shall watch over her, and she shall be as well protected as if an army of ten thousand men closed its bayoneted wall around her. Moreover, for the next four days, she will be in no danger whatever - her unknown friend has informed us of this - and on the fifth day, yes, I will lay her enemies, shattered into atoms, at her feet as a token of my deep reverence and devotion."

I opened my eyes wide. Holmes stood before me in a completely new guise, a knight, a hero, with the air of a poet and troubadour. Only his self-conscious superiority was the same as usual.

However, Mrs Whalters was hesitant.

"Shouldn't we be travelling anyway?"

Holmes didn't have to answer; another, Dar Mila, did it in his place.

"We are staying. When he says he's protecting us, we can't be in any danger."

Against Her Highness's stated decision, there was no choice. Mrs Whalters agreed to stay. Shortly afterwards, we broke up. With a charming smile, Dar Mila extended her hand to Holmes, a favour I completely missed. Women are often so strange; who can understand them? I have been married for two years; for the first three months, I thought I knew every corner of Mrs Watson's beautiful soul; after a year, I found that her mind, her temperament, her likes and dislikes had whole provinces of which I had never dreamed, and now she seems to me more like a map of Africa of the 1830s, with only the extreme edge of the coasts marked, all the rest being unknown country. All I know is that there are volcanoes there.

Mrs Whalters followed us down the stairs.

"Oh, Mr Holmes! How glad I am to know your opinion of the woman! All my limbs tremble when I think that it might have been someone other than you to whom Dar Mila spoke as she spoke to you. It was a complete declaration of love. I thank God that your breast is girded with a sevenfold armour against woman and love. But poor little Dar Mila! Oh, Mr Holmes! I, too, have known hopeless lovesickness - that was before I knew my covetous John. Poor Dar Mila! And she who rejected a lord!"

*

FOR two whole days I did not hear from Sherlock Holmes. On the morning of the third day, I sat in my consulting room waiting for patients who unfortunately did not turn up. At 12 o'clock, however, a person came to seek help, apparently a rich man whose healing can make a doctor's reputation. He was excessively fat, with a red, swollen face and a grey beard.

"Doctor, help me!" he moaned hoarsely. "I'm having such a hard time breathing - asthma, you see."

"I understand, and I'm sorry," I said sympathetically. "Your case is obviously difficult, but I'm sure we'll find a cure. I've had a lot of asthma patients and always managed to cure them."

This statement was hardly in line with reality - I had my first case of this kind in front of me - but a doctor's duty is to encourage his patients.

I asked the usual questions and was about to start with the usual physical examination, when the patient suffered a terrible choking attack, forcing me to go to the medicine cabinet to get some medicine. When I turned round again, it was Sherlock Holmes sitting in the patient's seat.

"Hahaha!" He laughed. "I fooled you again, Watson, but don't look so angry about it. You'll be seeing me in a lot of disguises in the near future, because Moriarty's henchmen are on my tail, and I have no desire to let them see my cards."

"How is the deal with the professor going?"

"Excellent. He feels the noose tightening around his neck; I can tell because he is beginning to resort to desperate measures. Have you read the morning papers? No, I haven't. Then read this!"

He grabbed a newspaper from my desk, pointed to a place in the news section, and I read.

"Uncertainty in London is increasing. We give some examples. A certain Mrs Somrith, on her way to do some household shopping, was struck by a brick falling from a scaffold and injured in the shoulder; in the vestibule of Mr Blair's bank, a person was robbed; a fourteen-year-old boy was assaulted in the open street, dragged into an alley and beaten for no reason at all; the local mail coach collided with a brewery vehicle, a mailbag inexplicably disappearing. There are also reports of other acts of violence, but we have no reliable information on them. All the examples are taken from a small and usually quiet neighbourhood, Baker Street and its immediate surroundings, and the crimes were all committed in the last two days. It is a disgrace that this can happen in the heart of London. What are the police doing?"

So I read. Holmes laughed.

"What are the police doing? Sleeping, of course, it always does. But do you know who were the targets of the attacks? The brick fell on my landlady; the; the man in the vestibule was Ralf Creekson, my agent; the fourteen-year-old is the head of my street battalion, and the mail van left from the post office where I usually deliver my mail. It was all about me, or rather, my Moriarty papers. The professor realises that I have reason to move them, having discovered where they were kept in my safe, and he has everyone who leaves my house and might possibly have the papers with them investigated - unnecessarily harshly, I think. But I play along with him. Today, I have visited nine banks and deposited sealed packages. Mr Moriarty can assume that one of the packages contains the papers he wants so badly to get his hands on, but he'll have to work if he's going to examine the contents of nine bank vaults."

My friend's body shook with his silent laughter. After a short silence, he continued:

"Now you understand, Doctor, why I came here in disguise. I wanted to spare you. If Moriarty's spies had seen me enter your room, they suspected that I might leave the papers with you. They have fine noses and open eyes. Therefore, if I were you, Watson, I would sleep tonight with only one eye open and my revolver in my hand. Perhaps you had better sleep in a hotel, for the professor might like to repeat his dynamite experiment here, and with better success. Be on your guard!"

I have said before that being a friend of Sherlock Holmes is not an unalloyed joy, and the prospect of waking up with a knife to the throat or being thrown 100 feet in the air did not particularly appeal to me. I couldn't help but ask:

"Then why did you come here, sir?"

Holmes raised his eyebrows in surprise.

"Out of friendship, of course. Why else? I wanted to talk to you, my friend. A man cannot be satisfied by merely chasing criminals, doing test tubes and staring at books. She is not only nerves and brain - these belong to her lower organism - she also has a higher, spiritual, ideal nature. She needs something for this too, something to warm her heart, something to fill and lift her immortal spirit."

I sat stunned. Was that Sherlock Holmes talking like that, Holmes, the advocate of the brain?

"You are a materialist, Watson," he continued, "but you are wrong. We Europeans boast of our superiority to the peoples of other continents - it is a chimera, a folly. We have developed our brains at the expense of our other faculties; we have starved imagination, enthusiasm, romance, and the joy of living; therefore, we have starved imagination, enthusiasm, romance, and the joy of living; therefore, they are with us, stunted dwarfs. We despise the East, for example, although it is basically far above us; it has what we lack: imagination, mysticism, the heat of blood, and unreserved devotion. I love the East. I would like to live there among swaying palms, in the mystic shadow of strange temples, letting my spirit sink into ethereal dreams, while my eye is intoxicated by the marvellous dances of temple dancers."

"Temple dancing shoes?" I interjected. "You who hate women."

"The women - yes, the woman - no! Woman, Watson, is the noblest product of creation. Man is superior in muscular strength - but the ox is even more so - man's perception is sharper in the lower spheres of life. But womana woman's body is a materialisation of the finest substances of the universe; her soul is woven of sunbeams and ether waves; therefore, her domain is the supersensible space of feeling, imagination, and sensation. I do not mean our women, the women of Europe, they are mere caricatures, cheap goods labelled 'cheap and bad'; I mean women as nature created her, women untouched by the corrupting influence of a false culture, as, for example, the woman of the East; she is the masterpiece of the creator's hand."

What was this? What words from the mouth of Sherlock Holmes! I was almost in doubt about his mental state. To lead the conversation into more concrete topics, I asked:

"Have you seen Dar Mila since last time?"

   FRANS OSKAR WÅGMAN

"I have met Her Highness," replied Mr Holmes briefly. His reticence teased me to say:

"She's half asleep on her divan as usual, right?"

My friend felt the sting and responded sharply:

"Her Highness is very interested in music, especially classical music. I have had to play half my repertoire of Mozart and Bach for her."

"Oh! You are holding musical séances at Cupperhill! You have quickly become very much at home in the house, Holmes. Perhaps you will follow Her Highness to Bandalore as her police and bandmaster."

"If so, Mr Watson, what else? I hope to fill these posts and, if need be, far higher. Ruled by a superior spirit, Bandalore would be an Eldorado, a model for all the decadent states of Europe."

Why did these words of my friend cause me such deep irritation? I never understood it, but that was certainly the case.

"You should marry Dar Mila and become that superior spirit who makes Bandalore a wonder of the world," I taunted. "You'll always have a spare moment to sit under the swaying palms in the mysterious shadow of the old temple ruins and watch the dancing girls."

Holmes didn't get angry; his thin lips just curled into a small smile.

"When I become prince of Bandalore, I will make you chief physician of my army; no man will be in any danger from that, for the Hindus never employ a European doctor."

"When can I expect my appointment?" I asked pointedly.

"Let's get the Moriarty story over with first, then we'll see. But goodbye, Doctor. It's nearly two o'clock, and I've been invited to lunch with Her Highness. Remember to sleep with only one eye open tonight!"

Holmes left. I cannot say that my reflections after his departure were of the most pleasant kind or particularly kind to him. He was, after all, such a shamelessly ruthless egotist. He had no qualms about subjecting me to burglary, robbery and murder. He was a fool. What was he imagining about Dar Mila? Idiocy, impossibilities! I've always had a reputation as a handsome and charming man, but Holmes... Bah!

*

ANGRY as I was with my friend Holmes, I decided to take his warning seriously and to stand guard, gun in hand. The result was that which often follows firm decisions. With my hand on my revolver, I fell asleep at eleven o'clock, and only woke up when the sun stung my eyes from a gap between the curtain and the wall. It was then eight o'clock, and nothing unusual had happened.

Another whole day passed without Holmes appearing, but the following afternoon he came in.

I have seen him in hundreds of disguises, but never had he looked so 'disguised' as now. He was dressed in the latest fancy dress, even his hair was coiffed, only the hawk nose, the angular movements and the chemical stains on his fingers remained as memories of the old Sherlock Holmes. I, for one, must give the latter the beauty prize. My friend had never been a particularly attractive man, but now...

"I am in festive attire, Doctor, and in a festive mood," he began, as effortlessly as if we had just parted with a hug and brotherly kiss. 'Congratulate me, Watson, I am the happiest of mortals! And for two reasons: I have Moriarty completely in the net - tomorrow it tightens - and tonight Her Highness Dar Mila becomes heiress presumptive to Bandalore and its chosen queen, my betrothed."

I got up, unable to utter a word. Was it the imagination of a madman, or had the world been thrown off course? Would Dar Mila? Oh no, Mrs Watson has been my teacher.

"My dear fellow," said Holmes, sitting down, "I understand your surprise and recognise your congratulations, even if you do not express them in words. What are words really? The manifestation of human inability. I have a command of the English language, Dickens and Macaulay did not have a single word in their vocabulary that I do not have, but can I express in words my devotion to Dar Mila and my pride in being able to say: my Dar Mila? What are words? Empty sounds. I despise them, I do not need them. My soul writes finer, more ethereal, more fragrant poetry than Burns and Moore ever dreamed of, but do I write it down on paper? No, Watson, no. I do not. - But hurry up, Doctor, hurry up! Get ready! Festive attire, you finest! You are my friend, my Bourienne, you shall be my witness at the solemn moment when I place my ring on the royal hand of Dar Mila. Then, when night falls, you shall see me crush her enemies to dust, and when the day dawns again, I shall go to my great work, the destruction of Moriarty, the last achievement of Sherlock Holmes, and then, Watson, in the words of the poet, my star shall shine upon other worlds."

I have a calm temperament, and of course, my friend's happiness was dear to me, but I confess that my preparations were not without several mishaps; my one shirt sleeve was totally destroyed, cufflinks broke like glass, and my moustache shaper became a single rag. Nevertheless, I finished and we went to Cupperhill.

I will not describe our dinner for four. I will only say that Dar Mila fell considerably in my esteem because of her lack of taste and judgement. It was most unpleasant to see her red lips touch Holmes's waxen yellow parchment cheek the moment he put the ring on her finger. Throughout the dinner, she had eyes and ears only for him. And what topics of conversation between the two! My friend's successful detective exploits - which, by the way, I would have told much better - the excellence of certain newly invented handcuffs and shackles - the inventor was, of course, Sherlock Holmes - narcotic poisons and sleeping pills, Professor Moriarty and the strange papers that would take him to the gallows. Such was the conversation at the engagement dinner. Holmes lectured like a private tutor, and Dar Mila listened as if he had spoken of the wonders of paradise. Mrs Whalters and I had to rely exclusively on each other, and I freely admit that she was extraordinarily amiable and attractive. She looked quite young in her party dress, and no doubt I should have preferred her to the Indian beauty if I had to choose between the two and a new Mrs Watson. She had that sweet warmth of womanhood which never denies its influence. Her devotion to the memory of St John was exalted and touching, and her understanding of some of the stories of my married life showed that she had a high intelligence and a sensitive heart. She had my full sympathy.

Even the end of the dinner did not interrupt my friend's discourse; he merely passed on to a sort of spectatorial lesson, lining up on the parlour table a whole arsenal of tools for burglars and detectives, and I watched with real disgust as the two betrothed, laughing and joking, fastened the shining shackles round each other's arms and hands. When Holmes finally began to demonstrate the papers so fatal to Moriarty, while Dar Mila leaned on his shoulder and with little girlish exclamations showed her interest and admiration, it became unbearable for me. Fortunately, Mrs Whalters shared my opinion.

"Doctor, let us leave the 'young couple' alone; their amusements are of no interest to us," she said, and we retired to the next room, where we were soon engaged in a serious conversation on the subject of marriage, and a wife's duty of obedience and subjection to her husband. I have seldom heard sounder opinions on the subject expressed than by Mrs Whalter's pretty lips, and I found it almost an unpleasant interruption when the coffee came in, accompanied by an Oriental hookah. Of course, I would have preferred to smoke a cigar, but Mrs Whalters thought it best that I should conform to the whims of Dar Mila - the Princess herself had made all the arrangements and prepared the coffee and pipe with her own high hands to give us a notion of genuine Oriental enjoyment. With a movement indescribably innocent and pleasing, Mrs Whalters opened the door of the drawing-room ajar and allowed me to look in. There Dar Mila was resting on her divan, and below, on a tiger's trap on the floor, my friend Holmes was stretched out, sucking with all his might on a hookah like the one offered me. When Mrs Whalters, with her own lips, took the first puffs from the pipe, I could not, without impoliteness, continue to protest. A few minutes later Mrs Whalters was sitting in an armchair, recounting in lofty terms, full of genuine feeling, episodes of her ideal life with her unforgettable John, while I, like a Turkish pasha, lay half-lying on a sofa, inhaling heavy clouds of a disgusting, perfumed Indian tobacco, listening less to the words than to the sound of my lady's sympathetic voice, until at last it seemed to float away into an ever more distant distance, and finally to disappear, while my consciousness was clouded and annihilated in the pitch-black nirvana of dreamless sleep.

*

WOKE up to hear my name being mentioned. I opened my eyes. Where was I? I saw a semi-dark room, but there was no one in it. So the voice I thought I heard was just my imagination. My head was heavy as lead, my joints numb, my eyelids closed of their own accord, and I felt an irresistible urge to go back to sleep. Then I heard again, now quite clearly, a hoarse, strange voice calling my name; the sound came from the next room. With an effort of all my strength, I managed to get up and staggered over.

"Draw the curtain, open the windows!" I heard the voice command; I obeyed fumblingly and mechanically; a brilliant sunlight filled the room, I breathed easier, my eyes and my thought became clearer, and on the tiger's fall beside the now empty divan, I saw my friend Holmes, but shackled hand and foot with the very same ingenious fetters whose use he had so eagerly demonstrated to her ladyship Dar Mila, his betrothed.

I had learnt enough of my friend's art to free him from his humiliating position. He got up, shook himself like a dog, looked round the room scrutinisingly, felt in all his pockets, looked at his watch, and then sank into a moment's thought. Suddenly he gave a shrill whistle and then burst out: "We have been asleep for eighteen hours. At this very moment,, they are far away in France, the devil knows where."

"Who?" I asked, surprised.

"You're an idiot, Doctor. Dar Mila, Mrs Whalters, Moriarty and hell and his ilk, Watson, we've been had like no human being ever has."

"Is the princess gone? And the sympathetic Mrs Whalters? Where have they gone?"

"Ask Moriarty and you'll find out. Doctor, what have I always said? Beware of the woman! She's always Eve in paradise with the snake behind her."

To go into further explanation of the matter would be an insult to your intelligence, Stig. Of course, it was all a plan by Mr Moriarty to get hold of those papers. With them in his pocket, as we learnt later, he had passed through Dover that evening on his way to Calais, accompanied by two ladies.

*

A WEEK after our adventure at Cupperhill, my friend Holmes came through my door. He was leaner and more yellow-pale than usual, and I had never before seen such an expression of bitterness on his face. With the single word "Read!" he threw a letter on my table. I took it, observed that it was postmarked on a Swiss train, and read:

"Oh, Mr Holmes! How well I understand your feelings when you woke to find us gone. It was Dar Mila's fault. She loved you so dearly and held you in such high esteem, but a fiancé who falls asleep at his engagement dinner - admit that this is putting love to too great a test! Besides, some pressing business called us from London, and Professor Moriarty was gracious enough to give us his company and protection. He is

now beside me, by the way, and sends you his friendly greetings.

Your beautiful engagement ring Dar Mila keeps as a memento of you and of one of the happiest moments of her life; unfortunately, she had no such gift to give, using as an expression of her feelings what was at hand: the dainty bracelets whose value you have so highly praised. As the 'Eye of Indra' and the dagger were of little value - Dar Mila had bought them at Tosty's bazaar in Liston Road - we have taken them with us; the dreadful seeds of the Evonistas bush you may kindly keep.

I sincerely hope that Sandar Singh's murderous league has not disturbed your peaceful sleep, especially as it existed only in Dar Mila's oriental imagination, as did the whole of Bandalore, the fairy-tale castle on the Rivaputra, the diamond mines, Dar Singh and Sandar Singh included. Even my unforgettable, dearly missed John has turned out to be a beautiful but sadly shapeless figment of my imagination, in reality taking the form of Mr Bob Shirney, a former partner in the colonial trading firm of Brookman, Shirney & Co, whose bankruptcy the other year caused a great stir.

The breaking of her engagement has had a fatal impact on sweet little Dar Mila. With life no longer pleasing her, she has renounced the royal throne of Bandalore and relinquished her dignity as a princess. However, Mr Moriarty hopes that she will regain her equilibrium of mind when she returns shortly to the music hall, an industry in which she has enjoyed real success over the years. Oh, Mr Holmes! If you ever read in the newspapers of the triumphs of Sara Bricks, "the beautiful Jewess", or of Miss Edith Sommermore, "the star of the music hall", or of Coralie de Brissandier, "the resurrected Judic" - dear child, there are many names - think with the kindness of little Dar Mila, who was once your Dar Mila.

Please convey to Dr Watson the assurances of my continuing deep sympathy. The glimpses of life within the hallowed sanctuaries of his home and his heart, which he allowed me to see, I shall always treasure in my heart alongside the memories of Blessed John.

An inner force impels me to write this letter. I must express my admiration for a man whose superior qualities of mind and body came close to elevating him to the throne of Bandalore at the side of the most beautiful queen. My tribute is of little value to you, I know. I am unfortunately of the sex which has no logic, no reasoning power, no brain, but I still have a humble hope that when you look down from your seat at the top of the dome of St Paul's Cathedral on the Pygmies crawling in the dust, you will remember with favour.

your devoted admirer
Dorothy Shirney
for a time called Lydia Whalters."

I put the letter down. There was a long silence. At last, I could not refrain from saying: "The Oriental woman is the masterpiece of the creator's hand; her soul is woven of sunbeams and ether waves. Is that not so, Holmes?"

"Ah, you quote, Watson."

"The European woman, on the other hand, is just a caricature."

"Like Mrs Whalters and Mrs Watson... yes."

"I guess I'll have to say goodbye to the post of Chief Medical Officer in the Bandalore army."

"Certainly. But you do have reimbursement in your large practice here in London, especially among asthma patients."

"It seems that your eyes, Holmes, will not too soon enjoy the marvellous dances of the temple dancers."

I would not have spoken the words had I realised the deep impression they made on my friend. He did not answer; pale, stooped, dreamy, far-seeing, he sat there, a picture of a defeated commander, a Napoleon after Waterloo. Then suddenly, he looked up, his features took on colour, his eyes fire, and with his old energy, he uttered the prophetically dark words:

"I have lost my battle, but I have won more than that: I have met the woman on my way!"

I sat dumbfounded. What did my friend Holmes mean? He is always great, but always obscure.

*

THE Doctor had finished his story, and I had seen Sherlock Holmes in a new light. I promised myself that the world would see him that way, too. It is my duty to restore the reputation of a misunderstood and underrated hero.

4. A comedy in the countryside

DR Watson! Dear friend!

I have waited long and in vain for news from you. I am impatient to hear new stories about the life of our mutual friend, Sherlock Holmes.

Your devotee,

Sture Stig.

MR Sture Stig!

You are like a blast furnace, constantly hot and always demanding more fuel for the fire. You realise I'm joking, right? I am always humorous. I am sending you two stories from my friend's experiences. They really show him in a new light. One shows his good heart; the other highlights the truth that even the most well-ordered intellect has its weak points and that the power of mysticism is great. Let us not judge our neighbour harshly!

Perhaps you will remark that I myself play too great a part in the first story, which should have led me to hide it "in the night of oblivion". However, it is not vanity that has led me to preserve it for posterity - after reading it, you will understand why. I am Holmes' historian, my duty is to paint his picture honestly and completely, and I know of no incident in his life that shows a similar character trait. Therefore I tell it.

Honour to whom honour is due! You should draw the attention of your Swedish readers to the fact that it is I, Dr Watson, and not you, Mr Stig, who is the narrator and appears under the simple 'I'.

In all haste, your

Watson

No doubt you have seen, as I have, the touching cartoon of an episode in the Boer War, in which the commander-in-chief of the English army, Lord Roberts, sits at a table in a simple farmhouse with a child on his lap, a little Boer girl, to whom he tells stories about the pictures in a book. The hero and victor of so many battles has forgotten for a few moments the tumult of war and the responsibility of his high calling to be just a man, a man with a tender heart.

My friend Sherlock Holmes is a hero as well as Lord Roberts, a victor in hundreds of battles against crime and evil; his laurel wreath is as well deserved as that which adorns the Lieutenant-General of England. A great number of accounts of my friend's exploits, performed with the weapons of wit and sagacity, are preserved by me for posterity; we know the man, as it were, armed in mail and sword, but we know little of the man with the kindly mind and the helpful hand. I want to make him known by drawing an idyll 'between the battles'.

*

BY his intervention my friend had succeeded in clearing Sir Joshua Redvick of a charge as undeserved as it was dangerous. Sir Joshua was not one to forget a favour, and time and again, he had invited my friend and me to visit his home, though circumstances prevented us. It was not until June that Mr Holmes could make up his mind to accept the kind invitation, and I went along as usual.

The mansion was in an unusually beautiful location; Sir Joshua was a gracious host and, despite being a bachelor, kept quite a large house and a good table; the summer was warm and beautiful, the nearby river was rich in fish, and we had total freedom with the only condition of punctuality at the dinner table; in short, we lived a truly ideal life of freedom, pleasure and dolce far niente.

We had spent half a week in the place, when one afternoon, my friend and I were sitting in our common parlour with a book in our hands, but really enjoying the pleasantly drowsy state that follows a good lunch in summer heat and idleness. A faint knocking disturbed our siesta. On our "come in," the door opened, and into the room stepped a young girl, barely 20 years old. She was obviously of the lower middle class, although her attire showed an effort to be as much of a "fine lady" as possible. She was dressed for a party, perhaps a little too ostentatiously, and showed both a certain naive taste and a little vanity. But to such vanity the girl undoubtedly had some right; she was very pretty with her dainty sun-browned face, her little snub nose, her innocent blue eyes, and her somewhat chubby but shapely figure; she was simply a little country Venus.

Very carefully, she closed the door and then stood there, flushed and embarrassed, unable to get a word out.

Holmes' patience is short under normal circumstances, but when does the power of female beauty deny itself? With unusual gentleness, my friend said: "My child, whom do you seek?"

"Mr Holmes," the girl replied.

"It's me."

"I know that. I know both you and the doctor."

"What do you want from me, Miss?"

"I wanted - so badly - so badly - to talk to you," the girl stammered in embarrassment.

"Well, sit down, my friend!"

She sat down mechanically on the edge of a chair.

"Now tell me your business!"

The girl was obviously fighting an internal battle. She had something on her mind that was hard to reveal or hard to express, twisting her parasol back and forth and picking at the fingertips of her grey gloves, all the while her eyes remained fixed on the floor. Finally, after a long pause, the words came: "Mr Holmes, I am so upset."

Holmes pricked up his ears, suddenly interested. "What's happened? Is it theft?"

"No, it's not."

"Maybe robbery and murder?"

"No, Mr Holmes."

My friend's patience was really being tested too hard and was running out. "What is it then? Speak up, Miss! What kind of accident has befallen you?"

I really felt sorry for the little one; she was so sweet in her blushing modesty, especially when, like a frightened child, she burst into a series of sobs, between which she squeezed out the words:

"I like - so much - John - Martens."

Holmes has to smile. "Well, it's no accident."

"Yes, it is, sir!"

"Why?"

"Because John - doesn't - like - me - anymore." To confirm the magnitude of the accident, large tears began to roll down her round cheeks.

"I'm afraid," said Holmes sympathetically, "that John has bad taste or is a bad chap."

My friend should not have said that. With a violent movement, the girl pulled out her handkerchief and resolutely wiped away her tears. "No, he's not, John's a great guy," she replied with exasperated energy. "He's really good. It's just that he doesn't like me like he used to."

"But what do you think I can do about it?"

"Help me."

"For what?"

"That John likes me."

"How can I do that when John is so stupid that he won't do it on his own? That's not my area of expertise."

"You've helped Sir Joshua out of trouble, and you've done so many other marvellous things - it's in the doctor's books - you can do anything you want."

No man is insensible to flattery; flattery has the properties of champagne to go to the head. Holmes was human, and his interest in the little rural Venus grew greatly.

"You think so?" He said. "It would be a shame to disappoint such a beautiful faith. I suppose we must try if we can."

"We will succeed," the girl replied with all the confidence of a strong nature. "I could have done it myself, if it hadn't been for that Rowena."

She mentioned the name with all the disgust a human voice can express.

"Who is Rowena?"

"Sir Joshua's first maid."

"Ah, then I know who she is," said Holmes.

"But, my dear Miss, calm down and tell me everything simply and calmly, so that I can assess the situation and draw up a plan to restrain the stubborn John and bring him to the right crib."

The girl smiled beautifully. "You are a real old dear, sir. As you say, I'd better tell you everything. But you mustn't look at me, and you mustn't look at the doctor either, or I shall be so embarrassed."

She began her statement.

"My father is the miller in the mill, a mile up the river. His name is Miller - a fitting name for a miller, isn't it? He's saved up a lot of money, and I'm his only child, sir, and my mum died when I was fourteen. My name is Sally, Sally Miller. Two years ago, I got to know John Martens. You wouldn't believe how handsome he is! He's got those light brown, beautiful eyes that go right down to the soul, and curly hair, and he's kind as gold, and faithful."

"Oh, fidelity is all right," interrupted Holmes. "I thought you implied that he was rather volatile with you."

"He can't help it, it's all that horrible Rowena's fault," Sally replied with a snap of her neck.

"Probably. All the evil in the world comes from the woman, Miss; she is the serpent in paradise."

"Very true, Mr Holmes. Rowena is a real snake. You are quite right."

"Continue your statement, Miss. You mentioned John Martens."

"Yes, sir, I did, and you wouldn't believe how handsome he is when he walks into the pew on Sundays in his grey suit and blue polka dot tie. And so he can look at you over the hymnal! You feel it deep down in your chest, so that it almost hurts, and the altar and the priest and the whole church start dancing round before your eyes. And if he follows you home after a party and takes your hand, sir, then it's..."

"My child," my friend interrupted again, "I'm afraid we're getting into too much detail. We must get to the point, you see. Who is the extraordinarily charming John Martens?"

"The second gardener here at the manor."

"I've noticed him. Slightly below average height, slim and lithe, with long arms."

"Oh, not so long, sir; they reach just round my waist. But agile he is. You should have seen him when he..."

"Save the details, please! Well, he liked you?"

"If he did! You bet he did. He was crazy about the smallest part of my little finger ever since the market in Longpuddle two years ago. He talked about love, and was so insistent on talking to father that I gave in, and he talked to father, and father said he thought he might have a richer son-in-law, but wouldn't interfere if Sally liked John, and I certainly did, gentlemen."

"And still do?"

"Oh yes, so very much, and much more since that awful Rowena took him from me."

"When did this happen?"

"In the spring. She came to the manor in the autumn and immediately began to lay out her hooks for John. But it did not succeed till late winter; then, John's visits to the mill began to be more and more infrequent. He was dull and did not seem nearly so fond as before, and the talk of weddings ceased altogether. Alas, Mr Holmes, how many nights I cried my pillowcase wet for John's sake, or rather for that tramp, who thinks herself better and finer than another, because she has lived in London, and worked for fine people, and has a hat bought in town, and talks more than we in the country can imitate. But is she better and finer and more beautiful than me, Mr Holmes?"

"Oh, she can't believe it herself. She hasn't got your pretty eyes, Miss."

"No, she has not, sir."

"Nor those cute dimples in your cheeks."

"Not a hint of it."

"She completely misses your healthy, blooming skin."

"She does. I've always said she looks like a whitewashed church wall."

"She has a rather petite figure, but yours is fuller."

"That's right, sir. But about the waist I'm rather thin. John always thought so."

"Of course, you are a much better party."

"You speak very truly, Mr Holmes. Rowena is as poor as a church mouse; she spends all she has and gets on collars and cuffs and hats and dresses and brooches and all that sort of thing."

"Well, Miss Miller, all things considered, I think your chances can't possibly be bad. You have all the advantages on your side. All that is needed is to open John's eyes; we must operate on them."

Sally jumped up. "Don't touch them with any knife, sir! I will never allow it. Whatever happens, you must not touch his eyes. I'd rather Rowena had him."

"Children," said Holmes, smiling, "calm down. No one is going to touch a hair on John's head. I was only speaking figuratively."

Sally sat down. "I'm sorry, sir. I thought you wanted to take him to the hospital and put him on the operating table and stab him with the knife, like they did with the Reverend when he had his stomach problems. I'm glad I misunderstood."

"Dear Miss, I only meant that we must open John's eyes to your personal merits, as he is becoming a little myopic about them. You see, human nature is such that you covet what you don't have, but you despise what you do have, and then value it more highly when you are in danger of losing it."

"Quite right, Mr Holmes. I was incredibly jealous of Netty Largent for her red coral necklace - I thought no ornament in the world could compare with it, but when I got one like it from my father for my birthday and wore it for six weeks, I threw it in my drawer and thought it was really ugly. A couple of months ago, I lost it, and now I often think of it with regret."

"You have good judgement, Miss, and that's just what you need. You are to John what the coral necklace is to yourself. John has thought himself too sure of you, therefore you have lost in value to him. Now, we must make him believe that he is in danger of losing you; that will teach him to appreciate your merits. We'll arrange a little comedy to arouse John's jealousy; we'll have somebody pretend to like you, to 'bat' for you, Miss, and you must pretend that you are not altogether indifferent to this somebody; do you understand?"

"I see: John will be jealous. It will be fun to see him walking around with glowing eyes and clenched teeth. But that 'liking' thing is only supposed to be pretend, right?"

"Just pretending, of course."

"Yes, because otherwise I'm not in it. I just like John."

"The question now," said Holmes thoughtfully, "is to find a sighing Celadon for the comedy, a person to play the part of the imaginary lover. You can't use any of the young country boys in the neighbourhood; they might take the game seriously."

"I'm afraid so, Mr Holmes; they have a good disposition for it."

"One of the servants at the manor? Not good enough. John would consider them too inferior rivals. The butler is too old. Sir Joshua? Probably not persuadable. So that just leaves the doctor and me. What do you think of me as a pretend lover?"

"I don't think John would mind," Sally replied diplomatically. Holmes laughed.

"I fear you are right. Well, then, it's settled: the doctor will have to take on the role. What do you say to that, Miss?"

Sally scrutinised me from head to toe; finally, the verdict was: "It'll do."

I must say that Holmes often treated me with a rather ruthless nonchalance, disposing of me as if I were a parcel. This time, too, and I protested.

"I reserve the right, Holmes, not to get involved in this nonsense."

"Nonsense?" my friend repeated, offended. "Do you call my arrangements foolishness, sir? Is it foolish to do a good deed, to reconnect two people who love each other but have been separated by unfortunate circumstances? You are hard, Watson; you have no heart; you are an egoist, a selfish creature. And selfishness is one of the ugliest stains on character."

His crushing words evidently gave Miss Sally a very bad opinion of me; she sent me looks which expressed both great contempt and astonishment. The weight of this double dislike was more than I could bear; I felt my resistance breaking down. But I still would not give in without some struggle.

"But Mrs Watson? Think of Mrs Watson, my friend! What will she say?"

"Nothing. She can't know anything. We don't play our comedy here to a full audience with tickets."

"Well, as you wish then," I admitted.

"The matter is settled," Holmes concluded. "The performance begins tonight. And now, little Miss Miller, go home and play your part as cleverly as your quick wit and the innate charm of the female sex will allow. Believe me: this comedy will end like any other: with marriage."

Sally got up to leave, but stopped, apparently undecided, at the door.

"What else is it, my dear?" Holmes asked.

"There's something I'd like to ask you about," said Miss Miller, embarrassed.

"And that is?"

"Is it necessary for the doctor to kiss me? I'd rather not."

"It's not necessary, at least not in the first act, and I hope we don't have to go to extremes."

"But I'll have to put up with him stroking my cheek, won't I?"

"It might be necessary - at least in the final scene."

"Thank you, Mr Holmes, for all your help and information!"

She disappeared. The comedy was planned.

*

THAT very evening, I took up my new role, and over the following days it occupied a great deal of my time and - why should I hide it? - of my interest. The various situations and moods in which I found Sally Miller were certainly conducive to making her interesting. Our little encounters took place in the mill's little garden - but only when Miller was busy milling - on the way to the dairy, or on the way to the village shop, when I once had to row her up the river. She did, however, strictly forbid me to meet her on the night she returned somewhat late from a party at her friend Netty Largent's.

After three days our comedy had proceeded in this way without any visible sign of the intended result; John Martens kept as calm and cool as the stones in the wall that surrounded his garden. My role also seemed less appealing to me as time went on, as Sally's behaviour was far from being as friendly and accommodating as I had a right to expect. In fact, she only talked to me about John and how he might act. Basically, she was exactly the kind of egotist she had considered me to be and deeply despised, but a cute little selfish one; there was no denying it.

When I met her on the evening of the third day at the dairy farm, she was depressed and almost unfriendly. "I'm tired of this," she said, "it's no use. John doesn't care about it, and Rowena is holding on to him by the skin of her teeth. We'd better stop, Doctor."

The look she gave me as she poured the contents of the straw into the big milk bottle was so reproachful as if it were I and not Rowena, who was keeping the beloved John away from his longing bride. I felt offended and replied as indifferently as I could, "All right, Sally, let's stop. It is not really to my advantage to play my part, nor to my pleasure when you are so unkind."

"Actually, you should say Miss Sally, at least when John Martens can't hear it; another thing is, if he was listening, that lonely Sally might ring in his ears. As for ending the comedy, we'll have to be patient, sir; Rome wasn't built in a day. And what would Mr Holmes say if we suddenly drew a line under his well-laid plan? It would be ungrateful to him, who is so kind and cares so much for John and me. No, doctor, never talk of quitting," she repeated with reproachful emphasis as if the suggestion had been mine and not hers. "But," she went on, "I have milked enough. You can carry the bucket through the meadow, but not a bit further. It might happen that John had the roads this way, and it would do him good to see you dragging the milk pail."

I "dragged the bucket" through the meadow and was actually very glad not to have to carry it "any further" - my education was not in that direction, and neither were my habits. I am afraid my stock in Miss Sally's favour fell far below par because of this defect in my upbringing. "I'm sure you've spilt a whole pint of milk," she said, scrutinising the contents of the pail with her eyes. "Not being able to carry a little milk without letting it spill over! John Martens could do it with his little finger." Rather ungraciously, she said goodbye, and I walked home, pondering the sage's words: another wasted day.

When I met Sally the next day, the cloud on her sweet forehead had cleared, and her face shone with the brightest sunlight. She smiled radiantly, showing her small white teeth between her purple lips. Then she took my hand in hers - a small hand that felt both strong and soft at the same time.

"Doctor," she greeted him, "I thought John had been at the mill. He came early this morning and made up an excuse to ask if Father had any window panes at home - he said he'd broken a couple of windows in the greenhouse. Of course, he knew Father didn't have any window panes in stock, but it was to see me that he came. 'Miss Sally' - he used the word, miss, sir, he's always so polite.

'Miss Sally,' he said, 'do you know what they are talking about everywhere?'

'What do you mean? I don't know anything,' I replied.

'Well, it is said that the red-haired gentleman from the manor house often sneaks around the mill.'

'Oh, he does, does he? What is he doing there? Is he putting herring in the pond, or is he studying the mechanics of the water wheel?'

'Oh, you know what he wants. He's batting for you; it's on everyone's lips.'

'People talk so much rubbish,' I said.

'It's not rubbish, it's true, I know it.'

'How do you know?'

'I saw him last night carrying the milk bucket for you, Sally, and he looked so delighted.'

I could hardly restrain myself from laughing, for I was so happy, first at the thought that John had really begun to be jealous, and then at the memory of your face when you carried the bucket - you were all well pleased then, sir? - But of course, I had to keep a stiff upper lip.

'Well, if it were, who cares?' I said coldly.

'I know one who cares.'

'Who?'

'I do,' he replied, looking reproachfully into my eyes.

'Careful, Mr Martens, I don't think that grief will be too hard to bear. It would have been different if he'd been carrying Rowena's rubbish bin.'

I hurried in, for I was afraid of betraying myself, as John really looked so sad, and I felt so sorry for him that I would have liked to kiss him, but I did not want to do so, because I felt that he was not yet soft enough to be taken in.

And now, doctor, you may give me a bouquet as a present, but you must see to it that Martens is the one who ties it for you, and knows that it is meant for me. And since you are kind today and not unpleasant as yesterday, you will have to row me up to the village tomorrow afternoon, I am going there to change wool and buy some spices."

The following afternoon, I took a walk in Sir Joshua's garden and found Mr Martens busy tying up the rose bushes.

"Good day, Mr Martens!" I greeted. "You're taking care of the roses, I see."

I heard some indistinct sounds that were probably meant to be an answer, while John continued his work with redoubled fervour.

"Speaking of roses, please tie a bouquet for me, sir," I continued.

"You'd better get in touch with the head gardener."

"But he has gone to the city, you know that. Please do as I ask."

Not daring to refuse, he slowly and reluctantly began to cut off some flowers, obviously, the ugliest he could find.

"Make it really beautiful and elegant, Mr Martens," I said. I could not deny myself the pleasure of tormenting him a little, for Sally's constant comparisons between me and him, exclusively in my dear John's favour, did not make my mind entirely benevolent. "Make it very pretty, for it will be a present to a pretty girl! La France, Folkestone and Monsieur Boncenne are the varieties I like best."

"I'm afraid, sir, that I'm tying a bad bouquet for you," he replied, with a clear emphasis on you. And he was right in his fear; I have never seen a more tasteless bouquet than the work of his hands. In revenge, I said: "There is a pair of beautiful blue eyes, not far from here, that will rest on your masterpiece. I can already see in my imagination how they will beam with joy."

He didn't reply, but with amazing energy started raking away some fallen leaves, while I made my way down to the mill to collect Sally for the planned boat trip up to the village.

She accepted the bouquet with delight. "He has tied it, you say? Isn't he pretty - yes, I mean the bouquet, of course. Did you hint that it was for me? What did John look like when you told him? John dear, were you very angry or very sad?"

She put the bouquet in a vase in the window. Did she kiss it on the sly? I think she did.

On the whole, the boat trip offered nothing particularly interesting - until the end. Miss Sally was taciturn and not quite in the mood. Contrary to expectations, Mr Martens had not appeared within sight of the mill during the day, and Sally, with true womanly logic, took his neglect out on me. In vain did I endeavour to display my, I dare say, not inconsiderable conversational powers; little Miss remained equally inaccessible and sulky, and I think she even nodded now and then in a quiet slumber.

Suddenly, her behaviour changed. It was on the way home, not far from where we were to dock; I was sitting at the oars,, and she was on the bench next to me, facing me. She leaned forward quickly and whispered:

"You can hold my hand, sir!"

I looked up into her face in surprise; what I saw made me flinch: her cheeks glowed the hottest red, and in her eyes shone a lustre not usually there, the hand that was placed in mine trembled slightly.

Suddenly, it was clear to me: this was the mark of passion. Had we been playing too carelessly with fire? Was the comedy threatening to turn into tragedy? Was all this coldness that Sally had shown me just the result of an inner struggle between duty and emotion, a cover to hide a growing passion? It had to be, it couldn't be anything else; everything pointed in that direction. I was a man in the prime of life, endowed with all the prerogatives of education and refinement, and my appearance had been judged most favourably by a few ladies in India; she was an inexperienced child of the people, of simple education, with a little habit of controlling her feelings, long without a mother's guidance, her mind, in consequence of the break with Martens, was now unusually sensitive and open to impressions, circumstances had brought her and me together in an intimate, emotional, mysterious relationship - what was more natural than that the young girl's heart should have begun to speak, to speak the expressive language of suffering?

To my honour, I can declare that any thought of exploiting Sally's weakness and playing upon her warm feeling was utterly alien to me; pity, heartfelt pity for her I felt, and deep anxiety as to how I should proceed to restore her tenderly yet firmly to calm and normality of mind.

She solved the riddle herself - she was very much a child of nature and had its fickleness and energy. While

I sat in my anxious thoughts, letting the boat drift fearlessly with the current, she hastily pulled her hand out of mine, got up and sat down on the far bench. To my puzzled question she replied only briefly: "Don't mind me!" and when the boat reached the shore a few minutes later, she quickly jumped onto the beach and disappeared without even saying goodbye.

I understood her well: she had triumphed over her own suffering - the greatest victory a man can win, and I honoured her for it. But this was the outcome of the present moment; would not the victory be turned into defeat in the days to come? There was in Sally's temperament a fierceness and strength of will that was more inclined to defy than to yield to obstacles. I lay half the night wondering what to do, and the other half was spent in an uneasy slumber, filled with dreams of Sally Miller.

I had not had time to get up the next morning when I was handed a letter without a postmark; a barefoot boy had left it. I recognised the hand that had written it even before I opened it, and I tore open the envelope with trembling apprehension and a shaking hand. What would it contain? "Poor little Sally Miller!" sighed my pitiful heart. The letter read:

"Doctor! You must have been surprised at the way I behaved last night on the row home, that I wanted to hold your hand for a moment and then sat so far away. Did you think I was mad? Well, I wasn't, Doctor, but I was very clever, as you will hear. I happened to look into the bushes on the beach - they are full of them, as you will

have noticed - and what did I see? Well, John Martens, creeping between them - he must have been following us for some time - and it immediately occurred to me that it would be a good thing if he thought that you liked me very much, but that I didn't like you - which is the plain truth, as you can testify yourself, sir. John was also standing under the big alder tree near the landing place, so I didn't want you to say anything, which is why I disappeared so quickly.

John caught up with me on the road and followed me all the way home and into the garden. He was so terribly angry and sad, and said he didn't care about anything, and that he would go to America or do some other foolish thing, just because I no longer liked him. When I replied that he liked Rowena more than me, he declared that Rowena was not worth a piece of the sole of my shoe - wasn't that a very strong word? - and when I spoke of Rowena's beauty and fineness, he insisted that if she were as beautiful as Mary Stuart, and finer than the circus girl at Richmond, he cared no more than if he had lost a hair. I was to him the most beautiful and the finest thing in the world. I felt so sorry for him, and he was so handsome and stately in his great agitation, and we were becoming real friends again, when he happened to see the bouquet you gave me, standing in the open window. You wouldn't believe how angry he got, he had a fit of real anger, jumped up on a bench and snatched the bouquet, which he tore into pieces and threw over the hedge into the ditch. Then he began to say that you would pay dearly for that bouquet and all your antics, so dearly that you would remember it all your days, and with that, he took off like a rocket, and I went into my room and cried so much that at supper my father asked me why I was so red-eyed, and I had to lie and make up that I had caught such a terrible cold.

I am writing this to ask you to be careful with John, so that he does not do anything stupid and get into trouble, poor John, who is probably in trouble anyway at the moment. I'll soon talk some sense into him and put things right - it won't be difficult, I'm sure. But don't come here, Doctor, under any circumstances, I beg you!

Yours sincerely

Sally Miller."

When I signed it, I made a curious observation: it had originally said 'Sally Martens', but the word Martens had been crossed out and replaced by Miller.

The letter fell from my hand. Was it for this that I had worried so much and sacrificed my night's sleep? Not even a simple thank you came to me. Through my head ran a stream of thoughts about the woman and her qualities, which thoughts, however, I do not consider necessary to attach to this story.

As easily as Sally wished, I was not going to be dismissed. I felt the need to give Miss Sally Miller a little lesson in consideration and delicacy; Mr Marten's threats I cared little for; under Sherlock Holmes's instruction, I had learned some good tricks which in a scuffle were useful and apt to put an opponent out of action. I jumped out of bed, dressed hastily, and went down to the mill.

I assumed that at this time of the morning, Sally was in the garden harvesting the asparagus beds. So there I directed my steps, but stopped involuntarily under the open window of Sally's room. What kept me there as if pinned down was the sound of a voice coming from inside the room, Sally's familiar voice, although I had never heard it with such a timbre as now.

"My dear John," the voice said, "you mustn't be sad any more. Everything is all right again, and we are all so happy and contented inside. I know that deep down, you have always and only liked me, even though that stupid Rowena tried to confuse you, and I can understand how you could get angry last night; you thought I liked the doctor."

"But you don't, not at all, not the least bit, my darling, my own sweet, faithful Sally?" It was not easy to recognise in the voice that now spoke the kinship with the one that had sounded to me the day before in the garden, but I could not doubt that the voice belonged to "dear John".

The answer was not long in coming. "My dear, you can't believe something so ridiculous? I should like that red beard, that dull fellow! Oh, one has better taste when one's name is Sally Miller."

"And soon to be called Sally Martens!"

"In three months, John!"

"In two, Sally!"

"No, Johnny - I haven't time to finish, sir. You want a pretty little bride, don't you?"

"Dear little Sally!"

"My own John!"

The voices fell silent, for what reason I could not determine with certainty. A few faint, indistinct, slightly banging sounds were the only thing that broke the silence.

I stood for a few minutes pondering the capricious play of fate and the strange course of life. Then I heard the garden gate slam shut, firm but urgent footsteps crunching against the gravel path, and the sturdy figure of Miller, the miller, in the white garb of innocence and his profession, stood before me:

"Oh, you're here again, you … you … well, I don't want to say what I'm thinking; I don't like strong words, sir. I saw you coming this way and followed you to read you the law properly once and for all. Is that the behaviour of a gentleman? Sneaking round my knots after an innocent girl who is motherless and whose father runs a mill? Is it, sir? Is it nicely done? Answer me, please! Is it right that you should force the whole neighbourhood to gossip about you and Sally, and make a fool of yourself, you old fool? Tell me, is it right? Why don't you say yes? One might just think you would. But listen, my dear sir, if I see you again in my neighbourhood or within 2000 metres of Sally, I'll dip you in my millpond and let you go through the gristmill. Now you know. A better man breaks his promises for Sally Miller! You won't, sir. And now goodbye! Go away and never come back again!"

I will not describe the state of mind in which I returned to the mansion, but I am sure Sherlock Holmes was made aware of his record of guilt for his insane idea of comedy, the source of all my humiliations.

My soul and mood only regained their usual equilibrium after dinner, when we sat with our wine and cigars. But suddenly, Sir Joshua asked me a question that reopened the wounds in my soul.

"Look here, doctor," he said, "what harm have you done to Rowena, my first maid?"

"As far as I know, I have never done Miss Rowena any harm or good. I have hardly spoken to her," was my reply.

"The housekeeper tells me, however, that Rowena is very angry with you, and has said that anyone who deigns to touch your clothes or brush your shoes should not be tolerated in the company of decent people."

"It's completely incomprehensible to me," I replied.

"But I think I have the key to Miss Rowena's disposition towards the doctor," said my friend Holmes, and then gave a full account of our comedy, its prelude and denouement, so that Sir Joshua burst into real fits of laughter.

"Doctor," said our host, "if you're finally going to play comedy, be careful not to choose a role in the play 'Between the Bark and the Tree'."

*

ONE day at the end of September, I received a parcel in the post containing an exquisite bouquet of roses and a letter. The latter read as follows:

"Dear Doctor! I want to thank you for being so kind to me when you were here, and for all the good times we had together. Neither my father nor my beloved John are angry with you anymore - they've found out about our little plot and are laughing about it. John sends you a bouquet instead of the one you gave me, and he tore it up.

Your Honour
Sally,
Who since 3 August is Sally Martens".

5. Harun al Rashid's Manuscript

"**W**ATSON! Fancy a trip to the countryside?" my friend Sherlock Holmes asked as he entered my office one fine summer day.

If I wanted to? Absolutely. And if I had time? Even more.

But there was one obstacle: Mrs Watson. My visit to Sir Joshua Redwick had had unexpected consequences. Somehow, Mrs Watson had found out about my role in the incident, and the information had been greatly exaggerated. As a result, she often let me know what she thought of my behaviour, my character and sometimes even my medical talents. Her statements were not very flattering to hear repeatedly. She usually ended her speeches by saying that she was going to move to 'Auntie Do' or apply to the 'Home for Abused Wives', but she never moved. On the contrary, she reduced her former frequent trips to acquaintances and was reluctant to let me out of her sight even for half an hour unless work demanded it. After each trip, I had to give a detailed account of the patient's age, position, residence, appearance and, above all, gender. I realised, therefore, that the proposed excursion would cause some problems at home, so I considered whether the pleasure outweighed the discomfort.

My friend saw my hesitation. "Mrs Watson has no objections, does she?" he asked with feigned innocence.

But I recognised the ironic glint in his eye. It was the typical look that bachelors gave married men. A look that says: "Poor you, having to worry about what your wife thinks." That look annoyed me, and I made my decision. "Not at all. How can you think such a thing? I'm coming with you. Where are we going? And for what purpose?"

Holmes handed me a telegram. I read:

"Mr Holmes, 221B Baker Street. London. His Lordship Lord Redmooreland requests your immediate attendance at his castle, Burgham Castle, for an important consultation. Telegraph reply. Stripers."

So we were to be the guests of the head of one of Britain's oldest families. I was to sit at his table and perhaps catch a glimpse of his famous museum, whose treasures were hardly seen by anyone but the owner himself.

I exclude the farewell to Mrs Watson—my colleague Goodwich promised on the telephone to give her nerves the care their torn state required—and the train journey. My narrative begins the moment my friend and I stepped out of the carriage that had picked us up at the station, and we had the façade of Burgham Castle before us.

The castle, built at different times and in various styles, was not very grand; it also gave a gloomy impression of desolation and lack of care. Immediately upon arrival, we were ushered into the library, a large, dark room with endless rows of books lined up on blackened oak shelves.

Two men were in the room. One was a slender man about 40 years old. He wore a suit resembling that of a priest and had a pale face. What was most striking about him was his unusually long and full nose and his calm demeanour.

The other man was leaning against the large marble fireplace. He held his hands behind his back. The fireplace was decorated with heraldic ornaments. The man himself was built like a giant. He had large, bulging aqua-blue eyes and a red beard that was so long it curled down his chest. The beard covered more than half of his shirt chest, which was not very clean. The 'billowing' seemed to be to the man's taste; moreover, the various parts of the garment had a spaciousness that made them fall into a heap of more fantastic than aesthetically pleasing folds and wrinkles.

As no one present made any effort to open the conversation, my friend took the floor:

"I am Sherlock Holmes. I have been asked to travel here for consultation."

The giant by the fireplace made some inarticulate sounds, almost like the growl of a bear, whereupon the gentleman with the plump nose said:

"His Honour is very pleased that you have come, sir. It was I who sent the telegram. I am Striper."

Holmes turned to the giant with a deep bow. "So it is his lordship himself whom I have the honour to greet."

Again, the growling was heard, this time as if coming from the bowels of the great fireplace.

So this was Lord Redmooreland, one of England's leading noblemen. How strangely fate can play! A generous nature had lavished its gifts on his favour in the richest measure but had apparently denied him one of the greatest: the noble gift of speech. I felt genuine pity for this unfortunate favourite of fortune - but I was hasty.

For just as Mr Stripers had begun to address my friend - "His Lordship wishes..." - he was interrupted by another growl, in which I thought I discerned the words, "The other man, what does he want?" - The Lord was not dumb.

Holmes hurried to introduce me; my Lord nodded a little and said almost clearly: "Speak Stripers!"

He began: "His Lordship wishes" - but was again interrupted by a growl, which the interpreter translated as follows: "His Lordship wishes the gentlemen to sit down."

My friend and I bowed but made the modest objection: "Not before you, my lord!"

Another growl. This time, the bear was teased and seemed ready to attack. Striper interpreted: "His lordship is used to seeing his wishes fulfilled."

At last, Mr Stripers spoke without being interrupted: "His Lordship wishes to hear your opinion, Mr Holmes, concerning an incident that occurred here at the Castle this morning."

"Please give more details," said my friend.

"Ben Perkins, the second footman, has his room in the great corridor of the ground floor near the gate to the courtyard. He was awakened this morning by a shrill cry from the corridor, threw on some clothes and went out to see what was the matter. As he is quite old and a bit slow in turning around, it took him a couple of minutes to get out. To his horror, he found Mrs Blondly lying unconscious with a nasty, bleeding cut on her forehead. He raised the alarm and set the house in motion."

"Who is Mrs Blondly?" Holmes asked.

"Our housekeeper, sir."

"Age, character, background?"

"About 42 years of age, very steady and honourable, has held her office for 13 years. She came here as the recent widow of his honour, Mr Blondly, assistant to the vicar of this parish."

"Where is her room?"

"In the small corridor that runs perpendicular to the large, third door from the garden gate."

"Where was she found lying?"

"Right where the two corridors meet, close to the wall."

"What did the wound look like?"

"As if inflicted with a blunt object."

"Time?"

"About half past four this morning."

"She was in a nightdress, of course?"

"In a nightdress? No, she was fully dressed. Mrs Blondly always makes a point of being neat and tidy."

"What did she tell you about it?"

"Nothing at all. On account of the shock and the blow, she was so distressed and nervous when she woke from her fainting spell that the doctor, whom we called in, declared that she must be left alone for a few hours. But Inspector Broome of Crapton, whom his Lordship summoned before he thought of telegraphing to you, is just questioning her."

"Ah, a police inspector is here! Oh, good. What sort of person is Ben?"

"A faithful servant, sir, slow but entirely honest."

"Which persons make up the household?"

"His Lordship's valet, two footmen, the cook and two maids, that's all, except his Lordship himself, me and Mrs Blondly."

"His honour is not poison?"

His Lordship had hitherto stood by the stove as motionless and indifferent as one of the savages who formed the shield-keepers of his coat of arms. To my surprise, it was he who now answered, and so clearly that we understood half of his words - the other half we could easily guess.

"Married? I want peace and quiet in my house."

My respect for his grace grew; he was clearly a man with life experience. More surprising was the addition he made after a moment's pause.

"I am the noblest nobleman in England; no one can boast so many ancestors as I; that is my pride. If I had married, I would have had a son; he would have had more ancestors than I. I will not marry."

What could we say to this? There was a moment of embarrassment, which Holmes broke by asking:

"Is the perpetrator of the violence suspected?"

"None," replied Stripers.

"No reason to distrust the officials?"

"Nothing."

"Has something been stolen?"

"As far as we can see, nothing."

"But why have I been summoned?"

"I told you: I want peace and quiet in my house."

It was the bear from the fireplace that made itself heard.

Mr Stripers clarified the meaning of the short speech.

"His Lordship knows that you are the most skilful detective in the world; you investigate in an hour a case which occupies the official police for a month. This morning's incident has disturbed the order of the house and His Honour's studies. Until he gets to the bottom of the matter, he cannot resume with the necessary calm the profound investigations in which he is engaged, investigations, sir, which concern nothing less than to ascertain whether the newly discovered precious tiara, with which his Lordship has enlarged his museum, belonged to a Median ruler or was seated on the head of the last Babylonian king, Assurbanipal. There you have the reason why you have been called here."

"No further information on the matter? Oh, no. Well, with his Lordship's permission, I will make some inquiries, the results of which I shall have the honour to communicate in due course."

My friend and I left the library. We had barely made it down the corridor when a small, robust-looking man approached us. The type was familiar; it was the official police officer.

"Mr Holmes, I suppose," he said in a good-natured, noisy way. "So that's what the great Sherlock Holmes looks like? Pleased to meet you, sir. And you too, Doctor, for so you are. You are inseparable as Siamese twins, ha ha ha! But you could have saved yourself the trouble of the journey, Mr Holmes. You're too late, sir. I, Inspector Broome of Crapton, have already solved the case."

"Really?" my friend said.

"Yes, indeed. Others than you also have eyes and brains. You can turn round. Everything is ready. I will show you."

The inspector stood right in front of us in a proud, military posture.

"There was an attempted burglary here between three and five o'clock this morning. It has been prevented by the vigilance and courage of Mrs Blondly. The offender is a tramp, rough, broken, drunk. I will describe the incident to you in detail, Mr Holmes. Just come along!"

He took us out into the courtyard, to the surrounding protective hedge, and on to each place he identified as the scene of events during his demonstration.

"See here by the hedge traces of a foot; it has been bare - the tramp has no shoes. The tracks lead from the hedge to the castle; they are not visible in the courtyard but are found here on the sandy path. They were made after three o'clock because at that time it started to rain and the tracks were made on damp ground, as you can see. On the threshold of the great castle door, you will again find prints; they are indistinct, but can still be recognised by the extremely misshapen big toe. They are not visible in the corridor - it is too dark here - but if I open this door, which leads to the dining room, you will see on the carpet the mark of the same dirty foot and the same distorted toe. The silver on the buffet caught the thief's eye, and he walked up to get his hands on it, but he didn't. Why not? He spotted the bottle of port on the buffet shelf, poured himself a glass and drank. How do I know that? You can see here on the rim of the glass is a red beard stuck to it. Just as he empties the glass, he hears footsteps in the corridor, gets scared and rushes out - he didn't have time to put the cork back in the container, as you can see - meets a woman, Mrs Blondly, who has heard the hall door open and has jumped out of bed to see what's going on. With a blunt object, he knocks her to the ground, and she faints - that's how she herself described it to me - the villain rushes out the way he came, jumps over the hedge - you can see the tracks leading from the house as well as those leading to it - and is out on the highway without being detected."

It was evident that Mr Broome listened with admiration to his own narrative. When it was over, he measured our insignificances with superior, pitying glances. At the same time, Mr Holmes stood silent and somewhat overwhelmed by so much sagacity, looking down at the carpet of the floor. For we were in the dining room, the door of which we had left open.

When Mr Broome had sufficiently enjoyed his triumph, he spoke again.

"There you have the case, Mr Holmes, the case to the letter. Mrs Blondly, of course, did not have time to take in the man's appearance, but I can describe him to you. I have called him a tramp; do you know why? You saw the marks of his feet: never in Christendom will you find the like of such deformed elephant feet except in the vagabonds of old England; they become such by constantly trampling the roads. By the way, the man was dirty - the marks on the glass testify to that - tall - he put the cork of the container on the top shelf of the buffet, sir - he had a red striped beard - the straw on the glass gave it away. It was a ghastly figure, a real criminal type, and a coward too..."

Mr Broome's story came to an abrupt and unexpected end. A voice from the corridor interrupted him with a thunderous roar: "You donkey, shut up with your nonsense!"

The words were perfectly clear, although the tone was reminiscent of a bear's growl. In a moment, his Lordship and Mr Striper also entered the room. And again, the former spoke:

"I heard what you said - stood in the corridor and heard the whole thing. You're a donkey, mister. The footprints are mine, and it was I who drank the port."

It was a long speech by his honour, but anger often makes people eloquent. But he fell silent, and his interpreter, Mr Stripers, had to explain further.

"His Lordship believes, Mr Broome, that you have made a mistake; you have allowed yourself to be misled by misleading facts. His honour is currently undergoing a Kneipp cure, which involves taking a walk barefoot in the dewy grass every morning. That explains the footprints. As the morning was chilly and His Lordship was upset about the incident with Mrs Blondly, he went straight from the walk into the dining room and had a glass of wine."

Poor Inspector Broome! So suddenly plunged from the lofty pinnacles of honour, he stood there petrified, a picture of humiliation and shame. I felt pity for him, but Holmes twisted the knife in the wound.

"I could have told you at once, Broome, that the man never came in from the highway; if he had jumped over the hedge, his heels would have been more deeply impressed in the tracks than the rest of his foot. And with your view of the matter, how do you explain Mrs Blondly coming out into the corridor fully dressed? With your permission, Your Honour, I will now begin my own investigations."

While he was doing this, I was served a delicious lunch in the library. Mr Stripers acted as host and companion. In the course of our conversation, I learnt that he had previously been his Lordship's schoolfellow at Eton but, for some unknown reason, had interrupted his studies. He ended up at Burgham Castle as his Lordship's companion and confidant, as well as spokesman and interpreter in all matters concerning the outside world.

After a while, our conversation was interrupted by the sudden appearance of Sherlock Holmes. "Mr Stripers," he said briefly, "how many employees does the gardener have?"

"Three except the assistant gardener."

"Have any of them left their positions today?"

"Not that I know of. We could ask the gardener. Why do you want to know this?"

"Never mind that, sir," replied my friend wearily, "nor talk to the gardener about it. I prefer to manage my own affairs on my own."

Holmes went as quickly as he had come. I saw that Mr Stripers was both surprised and offended by his snide remarks, but I knew that my friend was on the track of great discoveries when he displayed this temper, and I apologised to him, Mr Stripers. The conversation then drifted to the remarkable talents of Sherlock Holmes, and I recounted several episodes from our adventures together. I was still doing this when, after a good hour, Holmes re-entered.

"Mr Stripers, could you possibly get me a photograph of your assistant gardener Audley O'Reille?"

"I don't think I can," was the reply. "O'Reille doesn't socialise much with the servants in the house, so they probably haven't got his card, but maybe the gardener..."

"No, I already asked him."

"Then I don't know what to do - but wait! Maybe Mrs Blondly has his portrait. He is her nephew, after all."

"Is O'Reille her nephew?"

"That's him. Strangely, they didn't realise they were related until Audley had been here for a while - things hadn't been good between the sisters for many years. But eventually, the family feeling took hold - blood was always thicker than water. Mr Holmes, I remember seeing O'Reille's portrait on the mantelpiece in Mrs Blondly's sitting room."

"She's in her bed in the bedroom off the living room, I know that for sure. Mr Stripers, can you get me O'Reille's portrait without Mrs Blondly knowing about it?"

Stripers hesitated. "Perhaps that would not be acting like a gentleman. Does it have to do with your investigation?"

"A lot. Perhaps the solution to the riddle depends on it."

Striper pondered. Finally, he said: "Then I'll do it - for his honour's sake. I'll go in and see how Mrs Blondly is - the other housemaid's in there, so the breach of propriety isn't too serious; I'll take the photograph with me on the way back."

He left. Holmes was wandering in thought to and fro in the library. I dared not disturb him; it is at such moments that his brilliant mind produces its most brilliant ideas.

After a short time, Stripers returned and handed my friend a photograph. Holmes looked at it for a long time. Finally, his lips curled into a low whistle—the certain sign that he had made an important discovery. He placed the photograph on the table. "Open the museum, Mr Stripers!" he said briefly and commandingly.

"The museum?" Striper's features almost froze with surprise. "Impossible! No one may enter it without his Lordship's special permission and in his company, and he never grants permission except in the rarest of exceptions."

Holmes did not care for the other's agitated state. "Where is his Lordship? I want to see him!"

Stripers wanted to object that his Lordship was in his study and must not be disturbed, but the words stuck to his tongue. He realised that against this impolite, commanding man, resistance was impossible and contradiction a folly. "I will fetch his lordship," he said and left.

Soon, both he and his Lordship arrived. The latter was more than ever a growling, teasing bear. "You want to go into my museum? What do you want there? You won't be sticking your nose in there, I'll tell you that much."

Holmes calmly picked up his watch. "The train from Crapton leaves at 5.43, doesn't it, Watson? I reckon we've got plenty of time to catch it to London?"

His Lordship looked at him as surprised as a man can look. "What do you mean?" He muttered.

"Your Honour," replied my friend, with a reverence which, however, left not the slightest doubt as to the firmness of his decision, "I mean that either I shall finally accomplish the mission I have undertaken, or I shall abandon it altogether. Mr Stripers, would you be so kind as to arrange a carriage to the station?"

Lord Redmooreland was not accustomed to meet with opposition to his wishes; his eyes stared round and inquiring at my friend. Then he suddenly exclaimed:

"Stripers, get the key to the museum. It's in my writing desk, the third drawer on the right."

Holmes bowed, but Striper said:

"Your Honour, today is the fifteenth."

"Ah, you are right," said the Lord. "Very well, then, fetch the key from Mrs Blondly."

At these words, I caught sight of my friend's face and saw a feature that must appear in the countenance of a hunting dog when it scents game.

"Does Mrs Blondly keep the key to the museum?"

Stripers provided the answer:

"No, his Lordship has it in his own keeping. But once a month and always on the same date, the fifteenth, Mrs Blondly cleans the rooms - his Lordship does not entrust it to anyone else. Since she has to clean early in the morning so as not to disturb his Lordship during his studies there, she gets the key the night before. She got it last night, too."

"She has never abused this trust, I suppose?"

"No way. Why do you ask that?"

"Oh, it just occurred to me."

"Mrs Blondly is an honest person, Mr Holmes, and worthy of full confidence."

With this hidden reproach, Mr Stripers went to fetch the key. When he came back, he seemed really enlivened.

"You tried to cast a shadow over Mrs Blonde's honesty, Mr Holmes, but I can show you how unfair that was. Do you know where she kept the key? In her bosom, sir, between her body and her linen, sir. It had been hidden there all the time, in spite of her weakness, the maid told me."

My friend took the rebuke without saying anything but with a smile. In Mrs Blonde's clothes, I would not have liked that smile; it was not an apologetic smile, not an embarrassed smile, but the sinister smile of a detective.

"With Your Honour's permission, we will now go to the museum," said Sherlock Holmes.

Stripers unlocked the door to Burgham Castle's shrine, and his Lordship prepared to enter but was stopped by my friend.

"Excuse me, my lord, but it is important that not a speck of dust should be disturbed before I have made my enquiry" - and so great was the influence exercised by Holmes that his Lordship, like the rest of us, remained on the threshold as he entered the room alone.

The room was filled with tall cabinets and long tables covered with glass cases containing the museum's treasures. The cases were covered with protective blue cloth, on which a thin layer of dust was spread.

"When did Your Honour last visit this room?" Holmes asked suddenly.

"On Friday."

"So four days ago. And no one has had access since then?"

"None," the Lord replied shortly, and Stripers added:

"As you can see, Mrs Blondly has not been here either. She hasn't had time to dust today, which is natural considering the accident that happened to her early this morning."

"Gentlemen, you can come in now", my friend announced, and we entered. With real excitement, I waited for the moment when the glories of the museum would be revealed to my eyes, but it was not. Holmes had stopped at a corner of the table, carefully lifted the cover and revealed a glass box standing on an ebony base, containing a yellowed, damp-stained parchment, full of strange writing. After a few minutes of observation, my friend turned to His Lordship:

"This parchment is an antiquarian treasure, I suppose."

"One of the most precious treasures in my museum."

"What gives it such value?"

"It is a document of the rarest kind and known throughout the learned world: the death sentence of the Caliph Harun al Rashid on his famous vizier Jafar. No library, no museum can display anything like it, and the document is genuine, absolutely genuine."

It was certainly not easy to recognise in the man who was now speaking the bear that had just growled.

His words now flowed with a speed and clarity that surprised, and there was an almost tender undertone in his voice. His honour's soul had at least one soft spot: the museum and its treasures.

I glanced at the precious parchment, the strangeness of which I had heard reported in the newspapers, but had no time to make any further observation, for Holmes turned to his Lordship:

"I thank Your Honour for the information, and I am ready, at your request, to express my opinion on the events that occurred here at Burgham Castle this morning."

Was the investigation already finished? We all stood amazed at this, His Honour himself most of all.

"Are you clear about this, sir?" he asked with a hint of his old growl. "Not on the wrong track like that donkey from Crapton?"

"Your Honour will judge for himself after I have made my statement," my friend replied with dignity.

"Well, speak then."

"The account is quite long, and we can find a better place for it than here."

We went to the library. Once there, Holmes turned to Mr Stripers: "Would you be so kind as to send a messenger to Mrs Blondly, asking her to come here."

We all heard this request with surprise, and Stripers expressed our state of mind.

"Mrs Blondly? What would she be doing here? And she's in bed!"

"She is necessary for my statement. Please do as I say."

Stripers looked doubtfully at his honour, who shook his head:

"Mr Holmes, the less you have to do with women, the better. But you must have your way, I know that. Stripers, call the housekeeper."

Stripers, with the housekeeper, sent Mrs Blondly his gracious command. The messenger returned shortly with the message that Mrs Blondly's condition prevented her from complying with his mercy's request.

"Lucy, my dear girl," said Holmes kindly, "tell Mrs Blondly for me that she is to come here. Deliver the message verbatim, and tell her it is for her own good."

"Do you think the housekeeper will come?" Stripers asked when the girl had gone.

"I am sure of it."

Stripers smiled sceptically and shrugged his shoulders, but just then, Lucy came in and announced that Mrs Blondly would be there as soon as she was dressed.

We were amazed.

"I commanded, and she did not come, you ask, and she comes," the Lord muttered, and Stripers said:

"Are you a wizard, Mr Holmes?"

Ten minutes later, the housekeeper was standing in the library. She had a bandage on her forehead but otherwise seemed to be a strong and vigorous woman who wore her 40 years with honour and still had a rather pleasing appearance. The previous incident, however, seemed to have shaken her mind as much as her physique, and she nearly fainted as she came through the door. But my friend Holmes prevented this by pushing out a comfortable chair for her.

"Please sit down, Mrs Blondly - his lordship will allow it," he said in his friendliest tone. "I am sorry to have troubled you to come here. But you know that I have been instructed to investigate the unfortunate incident this morning and may need some information from you. And now, gentlemen, I shall begin my statement."

Lord Redmooreland took his favourite position by the fireplace, and the rest of us sat in a semicircle around Sherlock Holmes, who had begun.

"Two months ago, the position of assistant gardener here at the castle became vacant. It was filled by a young man, Audley O'Reille, on account of his good references and pleasant appearance. His behaviour did not contradict these good references either. Though not very skilful in his trade, he was willing, humble, and industrious. He disliked alcohol and seldom sought the company of others, but he was courteous and even friendly to all.

I told him that he was not looking for a company, which was true, but with some modifications. There was here in the castle a woman of better standing, impeccable reputation and mature age. Chance brought them together, and she discovered that she still had a warm heart in her breast. Many evenings after work, the two walked together in the leafy parks of Burgham Castle, and on Sunday evenings, young Audley O'Reille drank her tea in Mrs Blondly's sitting room. Who could blame him? After all, he was her nephew."

We all listened attentively, although we wondered where Holmes was going with these details. But suddenly, our attention was drawn from him to the housekeeper, who burst into an almost hysterical outburst of emotion.

"Oh, Mr Holmes, why do you say that? You know he was not my nephew."

"Yes, I know that."

"We said that just to be able to socialise without gossip... we liked each other so much."

"Calm down, Mrs Blondly," my friend consoled. "It was only a lie, and the world is full of them, in government, in church, in families."

"Everything was honourable and decent," sobbed the housekeeper. "We didn't even kiss each other... except twice."

"I believe you, Mrs Blondly; I am convinced that everything was done honestly."

Where did my friend Holmes get his power over men? There sat this woman, who saw him for the first time and confessed to him, to him alone, as if the Lord, Stripers, and I had not existed.

"I was so lonely, Mr Holmes. And Audley was so unlike Blessed John, my late husband; that was what drew me to him."

The female mind, who can fathom it? It has depths more unfathomable than those of the ocean. Thousands of times, I have heard women say that they fell in love with A because he resembled B, whom they had previously loved, but here, the liking was based on the dissimilarity. Perhaps the soil would have been just as fertile if the resemblance to Blessed Blondly had been striking.

It was I who made this reflection to myself; Holmes, on the other hand, took Mrs Blondly's remark as a natural thing, as something ordinary and regular. "And so you found amusement in his conversation," he added by way of explanation, "he had so much to tell you about London and life there and was, moreover, a well-bred and discreet man. His only fault was his obstinacy."

"He was not stubborn in general, sir, but very kind and docile; it was only in one thing that he was stubborn." Mrs Blondly almost forgot her grief in her eagerness to defend her dear friend.

"But he was even more stubborn about that," said my friend. "He even tired you out with his wishes to see the museum."

"It's true, sir, and I told him so. But..." she suddenly flinched as if a ghost had risen before her eyes? "How on earth can you know that, sir?"

His Lordship and Mr Stripers also seemed to catch a glimpse of the same ghost. To me, however, nothing that came from Sherlock Holmes was unexpected, and he himself continued unperturbed: "You did, however, resist all his entreaties, you did, Mrs Blondly. Only the day before yesterday, you promised him to see the museum this morning... it is the fifteenth, and you had the key to clean it."

"No, Mr Holmes, I promised nothing, by God, nothing, though he asked me so earnestly. But I did mention that I would have the key in my possession today. I did."

"And so he came this morning, at about four o'clock, I think, and woke you up by throwing sand at your window. You were displeased, but your heart was too soft, so you got up and dressed and let him in through the door of the little corridor."

"I was fully dressed, Mr Holmes, as I am an honest woman."

"I know that, and those who found you in the corridor can attest to that."

"Well, young O'Reille repeated his prayers, and in a moment of weakness - who doesn't have such, especially a woman with a tender mind? - you brought him into the museum."

"I did it, sir, and I shall always regret it and be ashamed of it," sobbed the housekeeper. "But he was so handsome, standing there all washed and fresh."

"You carefully lifted the covers and showed him the rarities. But he was not allowed to touch anything."

"He didn't get it."

"When he wanted to lift a glass box from its splat and take out the parchment that was inside, you rushed forward, grabbed him by the arm and forced him to let go of the box, whereupon you pushed him out through the door with a quick movement, which you then locked."

"No, sir, you do him an injustice, and me too. I didn't have to push him out; he went willingly. Would I have had the heart to lay hands on him? No, I threatened to shout for help if he touched anything, and then he left, and I locked the door."

"And put the key in his bosom."

"Not really. It was only when we got into the little corridor that he so stubbornly asked for the key. Then I hid it where no gentleman would take it."

"But he tried anyway?"

"He was furious, sir. He didn't know what he was doing. The idea of seeing the museum had completely bewitched him. If he had been himself, he would never have done what he did; he was always so noble and discreet."

"During the fight, when you were defending the key, did he give you a blow so that you fell forward against the wall's protruding moulding and got that nasty wound?"

"I think that's how it happened. He didn't do it on purpose, that's for sure; he didn't want to hurt me; we liked each other so much."

"Mrs Blondly," said Holmes solemnly, "you have committed a grave error in betraying your master's confidence and, contrary to his prohibition, in admitting young O'Reille to the museum. But you have an excuse: you had fallen in love with the brown eyes and red-cheeked face of a young man; such things have brought nobler and more intelligent women than you into far deeper cases. But at the same time, you have shown yourself a faithful servant: you overcame your weakness and fought bravely for your duty; you fell wounded but fell on the honourable path of duty, Mrs Blondly. And you have saved His Grace's most precious treasure, the parchment of Harun al Rashid, which was destined to be stolen. Getting this in his hands was Will Cruyk's plan. That's why he took employment here, and that's why he snuck into your confidence. For Will Cruyk is the man's real name, the name of one of the boldest and most cunning criminals of our time, the chief tool of the prince of all crooks, a certain professor whose name I will not mention here. O'Reille was only a cover, an assumed name."

Mrs Blondly almost fainted. "My God! Audley, a fraud, a criminal! I, unfortunate woman! What shall be said of me? What will become of me?"

"Calm down, Mrs Blondly!" Holmes said kindly. "For your essentially faithful performance of duty, his lordship will surely forgive your error, will he not, my lord?"

We had listened in breathless suspense to the conversation, which had thrown such a clear and unexpected light on the events of the morning. The impression was so strong that no one noticed my friend's appeal to the good heart of the Lord. From the stove came only a wondering, fierce growl, "Steal my parchment!" and from Mrs Blondly's seat a heart-rending, "Oh, I shall be shamed to death!"

Holmes rose to his feet. "Mrs Blondly, what you have done wrong will remain a secret within the circle that has heard your open and honest confession. His Lordship will retain you in his service - you have my word for it - and he will never be able to get anyone to watch over his property more faithfully than you hereafter. The feeling for the unworthy you will soon be able to tear from your breast. Go now to your room; you need peace and quiet - and allow me to accompany you there." With all the courtesy of a gentleman, he offered her his arm, and they both left the room.

Inside, there was silence until my friend returned. "My calculation was correct," he said. "All the servants were assembled in the corridor. They saw me respectfully escorting Mrs Blondly, which will disarm all suspicion and gossip about her."

"But how on earth did you know how it all happened?" Stripers asked. "You described everything as if you were a witness."

"Yes, how did you know?" agreed the Lord from the stove. "How did you know, you wizard there?"

"The matter is simple enough, Your Honour. Of course, I'll skip some of the details and stick to the main point. There was only one person known to be involved in the case, the housekeeper, so she became the starting point for my enquiries. I saw sand on her window sill, obviously thrown there by someone who secretly wanted to attract her attention; this was a man - through my magnifying glass, I saw on the protruding stone footing under her window the marks of his boot heels; they have five nails set crosswise; that man had climbed up on the stone footing to talk to her, and he was a gardener - down below the window is a bed of roses, and I saw the fresh marks of a garden rake in the loose soil; the rake the man had brought with him and leaned against the wall to have an excuse if anyone should see him there. The five characteristic nails had left their marks in several places: on the threshold of the garden gate, inside the small corridor where the housekeeper had fallen, and at the door to the museum - the limestone that covers the floor is soft and has a very revealing surface. So the man with the nails had been inside the house, and it was surely he who, for some reason, had inflicted her wounds on Mrs Blondly. How had he got in? Not by force - the door showed no sign of that - not by picking the lock - the key was inside. Someone had unlocked the door for him, and who else but the one who shared his secrets and was so intimate with him that he dared to attract her attention by throwing sand against the window pane, Mrs Blondly?"

"What was the reason for their intimacy? There were only two possibilities: criminal intentions or love - it's always one or the other when a man and a woman keep secrets from each other.

I knew the housekeeper from your description, Mr Stripers, so it remained to get to know the gardener with the five nails in his heels. As you remember, Mr Stripers, I asked you if any of the gardeners had left their posts today - it was not unlikely that if a crime had been planned and failed, the perpetrator would leave for fear of discovery and fear that Mrs Blondly would tell. Very true. After ten minutes' conversation with the gardener, I learnt that he was very sorry, and the reason for it: his young, pleasant, diligent and well-behaved assistant, Mr O'Reille, had left early that morning with his belongings packed in a suitcase. I could bet 50 to 1 that this O'Reille was my friend with the five nails. What did he look like? Some twenty years old, brown eyes and a pleasant face. Gardeners have an eye for beauty, but I dared not trust a man's judgement in this case and cautiously broached the subject with the gardener's wife, with the dairymaid, with Lucy, the maid; always the same judgement: the man was a handsome, proper boy, only too shy and fine, but then he was also the nephew of the housekeeper and thus of better family than the rest of the servants. I confess that this family connection puzzled me for a moment; it made my theory of 'love and crime' uncertain and flawed. It was then that I came to Mr Striper's and asked for O'Reilly's portrait. At once, all my doubts were cleared up; O'Reille was not Mrs Blondly's nephew but the villain Will Cruyk; his stay here was for a planned crime of great importance - Will never deals in trifles - the bond between him and the housekeeper was one of love on her part, of his intention to use her as a tool for the commission of the crime; but at the crucial moment Mrs Blondly had betrayed his hopes; there had been a fight, and he had knocked her to the ground.

What could the offence be about? Obviously something that was not available elsewhere, that is, something from the museum's contents. This was also confirmed by the marks of the five tacks on the museum door and by the fact that the incident occurred on the fifteenth, the only day of the month when the housekeeper had the key to the museum in her care. A glance at the room and the artefacts there revealed the whole scene that had unfolded before my eyes. A woman's hand had lifted the protective covering from some of the artefacts - no man would have handled it so carefully that the light layer of dust remained almost untouched, and I saw in the dust the imprint of a woman's finer fingers. But with the cover over the box with the parchment, the situation was different; there were marks of both men's and women's hands, and the dust lay in irregular heaps; the man's hand had also grasped the glass box and lifted it from the base, but had to put it down again in a hurry, as was evident from the fact that the edge of the box on one side was not inserted in the recess of the base. The dense and irregular footprints in the dust on the floor, some with the familiar five nail marks, indicated either a struggle or haste.

It was then clear to me which of the museum's artefacts Will had been commissioned to take possession of – the precious parchment; everything else was of no value to him."

"But, my dear Holmes," I ventured to object, "is it likely that Will would allow himself to be carried out of the room quite calmly when he was so close to his prey and then begin a struggle for the key to the locked door?"

"I, too, have asked myself that question, Watson, and found the explanation. Will did not dare to start a fight with the otherwise quite strong woman inside the room, which was filled with loose objects - any one of which might have fallen to the floor and made a noise. He preferred to lull Mrs Blondly into safety by acquiescence, and then, when she suspected no evil, to pounce upon her and seize the key."

Holmes fell silent. The rest of us also sat silent for a while under the strong impression of our admiration for his superior acumen. Stripers were the first to express our common feeling:

"Fantastic! It sounds like a fairy tale. And yet so simple and obvious. A real Columbus egg!"

His honour also expressed his innermost thoughts:

"You have missed your calling, Mr Holmes. You are not cut out to be a detective."

Holmes looked up in astonishment. Stripers and I stared at his grace with amazement. Such judgement at this moment, after the tests my friend had just shown! What was going on in his honour's mind?

His Lordship calmly endured our glances. "You should have devoted your gifts to archaeology, sir. What discoveries you would have made! You could have reconstructed ancient Babylon alive before our eyes."

My friend could feel his glory fully satisfied; in the eyes of his Lordship, there was no higher merit than that of being a distinguished archaeologist, except, of course, that of possessing most of the ancestry of the nobility of England.

"Your Honour entirely overestimates my merit," said Holmes modestly. "It is not nearly so great as you like to think. In this case, for instance, there remains an important, and for me, unsolvable riddle."

"But you've explained everything," Stripers objected.

"Not at all. The very core is still unsolved. For what purpose did Cruyk want to steal the particular parchment with Jafar's death sentence? Who was behind him as the original instigator? These are circumstances that, for me, are hidden."

"Will was probably going to sell the parchment as a rarity," I surmised.

"Nobody would want to buy it; nobody would dare to show themselves as its owner. There is only one copy of it, and the whole learned world knows that it belongs to the Burgham Castle Museum. If it were a less unique item, but Jafar's death warrant! My Lord, Mr Stripers, can you not think of a clue?"

Both respondents shook their heads. There was a moment of general silence. Suddenly, His Honour exclaimed:

"That butcher, Striper, butcher..."

Stripers looked at his Lordship quizzically.

"The butcher who wrote six months ago."

Stripers looked equally uncomprehending.

"The butcher or the brewer, the American, Burdhill or Drudhill or whatever his name was." His Lordship had been almost chased away.

Mr Striper's face cleared.

"Ah, your honour, you mean the brewer from St. Louis, Curvill, I think his name was. But he can't have anything to do with it; he's a millionaire."

"Wealth and morality are not synonymous concepts, Mr Stripers," my friend said. "Crime and millions, especially American ones, may well go together. Please let me know what is the matter with that Curvill, your honour."

"Stripers will tell you, sir. Speak, Stripers!"

"A few months ago, a letter arrived..." Stripers began but was interrupted by my friend Holmes:

"Was it a letter? Is it still there? Let me see the corpus delicti myself rather than have a summary of it."

"All letters to His Honour are carefully saved; I will get the current one."

Stripers went from word to deed, and within minutes, Holmes had the following letter in his hands:

"Lord Redmooreland! Honourable sir!

I'm sure you've heard of me; at least you've seen my labels with the blue rhinoceros, squirting through its nostrils a Niagara of beer in three golden barrels. The Rhino's beer is world-famous; all the fancy people drink it. The Rhino, that's me, sir. I'm the richest brewer in St Louis, that is, the heaviest man in town. Stratch, the meat packer, says he's five million heavier, but that's a lie, your honour; he lies as fast as a horse trots, though otherwise, he's a decent fellow and my good friend, though we play each other all the tricks we can think of.

I mention that I am a millionaire, but not to boast. I hate boasting and am not ashamed that my grandfather

- his name was Kurzweil, but I have Americanised it to Curvill - came to this country from Neu Strelitz as a shirtless tramp. I am writing about it just to show that I can honour my commitments on demand.

Last Friday, I took him to lunch at the Union Hotel - cover charge of $25, Château Lafitte at $18 a bottle. There were about twenty of us, all good men except Professor Ward, who is as poor as a church mouse - five thousand a year - but I invited him because I respect science and art - what would life be without education, sir? I subscribe to the Scientific Works - I have 39 volumes in gold on the shelf in my library and some other books as well - and I have statues, white in the drawing room and black in the hall - you have to make sure they match the colour of the walls, sir. Otherwise, there will be no harmony, and harmony must be there.

During lunch, I happened to say that you can get anything for money. Some of those present protested, the professor the most. I asked them to say what they couldn't get. Someone said: 'A clear conscience' - but that was not a fair comparison; it could not be tested. Then the professor said, 'Lord Redmooreland's parchment with Harun al Rashid's death warrant for his vizier.' 'Bet me six months to get it,' I replied. 'Top,' said Stratch, '50,000.' 'Top,' I said, '50,000,' and we wrote the bet in our notebooks.

That is the case, Your Honour, and now you must help me. Stratch must be deceived. I ask to buy the parchment. My bid is $50,000. For that sum, I think I could get a whole horse-load of old parchment from

   FRANS OSKAR WÅGMAN

New York, but I'm a gentleman, sir, and not a miser, nor is the wager a business, but a pleasure and a matter of honour; besides, it's Stretch who has to pay.

I suppose your honour, that you will accept, which is why I ask you to send me the old calfskin by return post, well insured. I laugh so hard I jump at the thought of Stratch's face as I unroll the parchment before his long nose.

Yours sincerely

D. Josef Curvill

P.S. I take the liberty of enclosing a price list of my beers and particularly recommend my porter: Curvill's best brown stout."

Holmes put the letter on the table.

"The answer?" he asked briefly.

The bear let out its most ferocious growl: "Told him off."

My friend sat for a few minutes in deep thought; then he spoke:

"Accept my compliments, my Lord; you have found the key to the riddle I could not solve. The fact is, no doubt, that this Curvill is determined to win his wager by any means necessary. He has contacted a person well known to me, the greatest villain, but at the same time the most ingenious man in both the New and Old Worlds and this person has sent his henchman Will Cruyk to steal the parchment."

His Lordship laughed.

"I snubbed him good. That Curvill will have to pay for his bet."

My friend remained serious, unusually serious.

"Don't be so sure of that, Your Honour. If the person I refer to has a hand in the game, he will not be deterred by an unsuccessful attempt to achieve his goal; he has hundreds of ways out in the store, and perhaps even at this very moment, a new attack is underway. Only when the time for the wager has expired can you feel secure in your precious parchment; it will then be of no value to the St Louis brewer and consequently to Moriarty - that is the name of the villain I alluded to."

"Would they dare...?" the Lord interjected.

"Moriarty will dare anything, my lord; to get the parchment, he would value your life no more than a rotten strawberry."

His honour was both surprised and horrified.

"What do you think I should do, Mr Holmes? Give me some advice!"

"In my opinion, there is only one way to secure both your life and your treasure: to bring the parchment to London and deposit it in the safe vault of the Bank of England until the time of the wager expires. Then you can put it safely in your museum."

His grace became almost lively.

"You are the guardian angel of my museum, Mr Holmes, tutor aerarii, sir. Your advice must be followed today. You are to take the parchment to London and deposit it, as you said. I dare not leave it in any hands but yours. And you will keep the certificate of deposit - it would be stolen here. Will you undertake the task, sir?"

"Gladly, my lord, to be of service to you, and I will return it to you - let me see: Curvill's letter is dated 10 March; the bet was made the Friday before, that is, 8 March; six months later is 8 September, today is 15 August - so in twenty-five days you will have your treasure again, my lord."

A few hours later, my friend and I were on the train roaring towards London. In Holmes's breast pocket was the parchment, well stored in a case of iron plate and sealed with the seal of his honour.

My friend was in the best of moods.

"This is the most brilliant investigation I have undertaken. Note, Watson, that it was not even known that a crime was planned, and I have traced its threads to St. Louis and Florence, where Moriarty is currently settled. My faculties and powers of mind are at their height, Doctor."

The following morning, in my presence, Holmes deposited the parchment at the Bank of England. The history of the parchment was over - we thought, but time would tell us otherwise.

*

I HAD not heard from my friend Mr Holmes for nearly two weeks, which prompted me to pay him a visit.

Without fail, I stopped outside his door, unable to open it. From there came sounds that almost chilled my blood: violin strings, two long ones stretched out and then a short one, cut off in incessant repetition;

always the same note, the same rhythm. I have heard the last act of Don Juan, the Damnation of Faust, and a whole host of demonic music, but what I heard now surpassed all in monotonous horror. At last, I plucked up the courage and entered.

Holmes sat at the table with his violin in his lap and his bow in his hand. The last time I saw him, he had looked like a triumphant man; now he looked broken. His head was lowered to his chest, his features were emaciated, and his eyes were almost lifeless.

"Dear friend, how are you?" I asked, horrified. He did not answer, just nodded absently. I took his hand to feel his pulse and, at the same time, stop the awful music.

"Your pulse is irregular, feverish; your physique is in trouble; you have overworked yourself!" I said in a doctor's tone.

"My physique?" he replied dully. "You doctors, why do you attribute everything to the body? What is the body? A dust, an illusion, a nothing. But, Watson, do you know the spirit?"

"My best friend..."

"You're a doubter, Watson, a materialist."

"I don't understand..."

"Of course not. The mysterious manifestations of the spirit are and remain a mystery to you. You are a doctor - that says it all."

"But tell me..."

"I have been a doubter just like you. But what did Hamlet say, Watson? 'There is more between heaven

and earth than your philosophy can dream of.' I know
there is."

During the conversation, my friend had become
increasingly excited. Now, he returned to his former
state of dull calm.

"Good of you to come, my friend. I must take my
leave of you. My time is short - down here."

I was beside myself with amazement and worry.

"What are you saying? Do you have thoughts of
death?"

"I've seen myself," was Holmes reply in a solemn,
sombre tone.

"Have you seen yourself?"

"Yes, and twice."

I sat there like a living question mark.

"My old confidant, the chronicler of my exploits, you
should and shall know everything. Sit down and listen
to me. Since my return from Burgham Castle, I have
been engaged in a very difficult and delicate enquiry.
The newspapers have told you that the hereditary Prince
of Abyssinia has settled in London to study English
affairs; he was for a time a model for young men, and his
governor, Colonel Glower, had an easy task. But three
weeks ago, the prince suddenly disappeared; everywhere
he was looked for, but in vain. Had he been murdered
or abducted, or was he in hiding? No one could guess
the answer. That's when they hired me. I discovered
that he had been caught in the net of a beautiful but
criminal woman and that in her company, he visited

secret gambling houses, but all attempts to catch him failed.

That was the situation as I hurried through the crowd outside the Stock Exchange on Monday. I was thinking of nothing in particular. I happened to look up, and five paces away, I saw myself, Watson, coming straight towards me. It was not a person who looked like me; it was myself. The vision lasted only a moment, then the figure or spirit or whatever you want to call it disappeared in the crowd, but I had seen myself."

I smiled.

"A delusion, a hallucination. You were agitated, overworked."

"No, I was calm; my soul was then in full vigour. I said to myself just what you are now saying, and I smiled as you are now doing. But I was wrong, just as you are now."

"Why?"

"I have seen the vision once more. I was sitting here in my room the day before yesterday, smoking after breakfast. Then I heard the door creak behind me; I looked up, and in the open door stood - myself - my face, my form, my gestures, my dress! I saw myself looking round the room, slowly turning round, disappearing and closing the door."

"Hm. Strange! How do you explain it?"

"Do you know what second sight is? You see your spirit, your other self. That's what I did. Do you know what that means? It's a death call, sir. Twice one may be thus called, the third time death itself comes. My end is near; I know it, I feel it."

"You make me more and more puzzled."

"My spirit is already leaving me; it is breaking free from the shackles of my body. Listen to me! I had received credible information that last night, the prince was to appear at the Commermans' gambling den. I wanted to arrest him there. I placed six trustworthy assistants in the neighbourhood with precise instructions, including not to leave their posts under any circumstances. At eleven o'clock, I myself would arrive, and we would set to work.

De la Noy performed in the evening at the Albert Hall. While waiting for the appointed time, I decided to attend the concert. The hall was packed, the heat was unbearable, the music was boring, and I was lost in deep thought.

After the end of the concert, at about ten o'clock, I went to Brixton Road, where the gambling den is located. Imagine my surprise when I found all my agents gone! My whole plan was foiled; I could not enter the gambling den alone; it would have been to risk my life needlessly. But my surprise was to be even greater.

I knew that Davy Snyder, my most skilful agent, and a couple of others used to drink their whisky and water in a restaurant on the Terrace. I went there, found them and reproached them for breaking orders. Guess what they replied: You came and ordered us to leave! They had all seen me, they had all spoken to me, I had given the same order to all of them, and they all confirmed that it was 25 minutes past nine. They are honest people, faithful and devoted to me; they have sworn to the truth of their statements and refer to the testimony of their comrades. Watson. There is no doubt as to the truth of the matter: while my body sat half-stunned in the Albert Hall, my other self, my spirit, was at Brixton Road wearing an image of my bodily skin. So loose already is the connection between my spiritual and my material being."

What could I answer to this? What would I think about it? I did not know. My friend's state of mind worried me deeply. Not that his mind was what is commonly called deranged - he spoke of all this with perfect calm and lucidity - but had not the superhuman exertion to which his brain had so often been subjected had a deleterious effect on his spiritual equilibrium?

His acumen, however, was as penetrating as ever; he read my mind.

"My mind is clear, Doctor; my spirit is in perfect balance; I am not superstitious, not a victim of the imagination. But I am a believer; I believe in the liberation of the spirit from the prison of matter. You are a doubter, Watson; therefore, you will never understand these depths of existence. I am called, and I am about to pass away; I have received the commandment, and the spirit is half liberated. It does not worry me and does not frighten me. But listen my friend, you must do me a favour: take care of the deposit of Lord Redmooreland's precious parchment, and if I should suddenly pass away, leave it in his Lordship's own hands."

Of course, I could not refuse this small favour to my friend. I took the deposit slip, put it in my wallet, and took my leave, clearly realising that Holmes wished to be alone with his thoughts and reflections. In view of his state of mind, however, I resolved to pay him another visit as soon as possible and, if necessary, to devote him to the care of my profession.

However, I did not have time to fulfil my intention because Holmes came to see me the following morning. It was my appointment time, and, unusually, I had three patients in the waiting room.

"Doctor," my friend said urgently, "I'm sorry to take up your precious time."

I cast a scrutinising medical eye over him. Fortunately, he seemed recovered from yesterday's hypochondria, although I could detect a certain nervous uneasiness in his manner. Perhaps he had fortified himself with some stimulating drink, for his cheeks were less pale than usual, his movements quicker, his pronunciation thicker and less precise.

"You never bother me," I said. "Please, have a seat."

"I haven't got time, Doctor; I've just come for that parchment."

"Ah, you've changed your mind! You want the certificate of deposit back?"

"The deposit slip?" He looked at me questioningly.

"Yes, the certificate of deposit from the Bank of England, which I received in custody yesterday."

"Of course, Watson. You'll have to excuse me for being a bit distracted today. Been up all night - the Abyssinia business, you see."

My friend's confusion surprised me. Had he forgotten that he had given me the deposit slip the day before? But Holmes always has his quirks, and I just said:

"How is that deal going?"

"Excellent, my friend. But I am in a hurry; the proof, doctor! I want to relieve you of responsibility for it."

"I am delighted. Here it is." I took it out of my safe and gave it to him.

"Thank you, Watson! You have done me a great favour. But I don't want to take up any more of your time, and I'm in a hurry myself."

He left. I was glad to see him so fit in body and mind and no less glad to be rid of the responsibility of guarding the evidence. What if it had been stolen?

This visit took place on Saturday, 29 August. On Monday and Tuesday of the following week,, I called at 221B Baker Street, both days without finding my friend at home, and on Thursday, I was engaged on a journey, from which I did not return till late in the evening.

On Wednesday, 2 September, I was sitting at my breakfast table, looking through my morning paper as usual. I was tired from the previous day's exertions. I was yawning heavily over the empty columns when suddenly I saw something that made me leap up from my chair and run madly around the room. Under the heading "Latest News" it was printed in bold letters:

Sensational news!!!

The famous private detective Sherlock Holmes was exposed.

He is a big thief!

The criminal is arrested!

My behaviour was so noisy that Mrs Watson rushed in half-dressed.

"What is it, Watson? Is there a fire? Is it thieves? Has the Queen been murdered?"

My tongue was paralysed. I could only point to the paper. Mrs Watson burst into hysterical tears.

"Why don't you answer? Have you gone dumb? What a misfortune; he has become mute! Haven't I always told you that your fondness for whisky and tobacco would come to an end with horror? Poor me! My husband is mute!"

I finally managed to get a word out:

"Read!" I said, handing her the paper and pointing to the place.

"Why don't you say something when you can speak?" she said reproachfully, then started reading aloud: "UK government bonds have been rising since Friday."

"Not there - there!" I pointed to the place again.

"So, 'The situation in the Transvaal remains largely unchanged...'"

I almost despaired.

"So use your eyes, woman!" I exclaimed excitedly. "There-there-there!"

My wife burst into a fresh flood of tears.

"He calls me woman! He is a beast. He is crazy! What am I going to do? Watson, it's all over between us! I'm going to live with Auntie Do."

Her hysterical outburst made me regain my composure.

"Honey, I'm sorry! I am not mad, but I am upset. Something inexplicable and unfortunate has befallen my friend Sherlock Holmes."

Mrs Watson's tears stopped abruptly.

"Is that all?" She said calmly.

"Just that?" I repeated reproachfully.

"He deserves a lesson, the unpleasant gentleman."

Again, my impatience woke up.

"But then read what happened. There, there, there!"

Mrs Watson finally found the right place and read aloud in a monotone:

"Who has not heard of the private detective Holmes? His friend, Dr Watson, has in a number of books thunderously advertised what he calls his friend's 'extraordinary abilities.' However, many, especially among our meritorious detective corps, have harboured a certain distrust of the man, his boastfulness, his arrogance, and his arbitrariness.

The suspicion has been realised far more than anyone could have imagined. But the pot goes so far to the well until it bursts. Late last night, Sherlock Holmes was arrested by the eminent detective Mr Gregson as a thief and possibly a forger.

According to the information we have received from credible sources, the situation is as follows: on behalf of

His Lordship Lord R., a well-known archaeologist and collector, Holmes had deposited a unique and extremely valuable manuscript in the Bank of England and was to keep the evidence of the deposit for the time being, but on Saturday removed the manuscript from the bank and misappropriated it, by what means is unknown, as Holmes, in the typical manner of hardened criminals, stubbornly denies having taken the deposit, although the bank officials testify to this and can produce the evidence. He has probably sold the manuscript for a high price to some dishonest collector.

The offence was discovered by chance. His Lordship's secretary, Mr Stripers, came down to London on 1 September to settle the Lorde's monthly account with the Bank of England, at which time the deposit was accidentally brought to light and the fraud revealed. Mr Stripers demanded an explanation from Holmes, but he could give none; he was innocent, and the proof of the deposit was in possession of his friend Dr Watson, a statement which was at once proved to be false, as the proof was in possession of the bank. On Lord R.'s telegraphic notification, Holmes was arrested.

For the day, we wish only to express our profound disgust at the hypocrisy of the criminal in pretending to act in the service of justice and our burning sorrow at the moral rot which seems increasingly to pervade broad sections of our people. Old England! What has become of your ancient honour, our honour and pride?"

She stopped. I stood aghast with surprise and pain, but Mrs. Watson said:

"A fine figure, your friend Holmes! Well, I always suspected something like that. He was so secretive and so rude. And then he dragged you off with him on nocturnal expeditions, nobody knows where."

I did not have time to give the indignant reply that was on my lips when a constable arrived with a summons to appear before the police magistrate the following day, Thursday, 3 September, at eleven o'clock.

Mrs Watson was beside herself.

"Are they going to arrest you too, my love?" she exclaimed excitedly. "Are they going to put you in an underground dungeon, let you be eaten by rats, die of thirst with a water pot out of reach? Tell me they can't do that! Tell them I'll defend you like a tigress defends her cubs! I have nails, Watson, real modern claws. They'll be careful. But tell me now - I'm your trusted wife - has that Holmes been teaching you to steal? Perhaps even rob and murder? Is that what you were up to during your secretive expeditions? Oh, I can see by your face that it was. Confess it all, Watson, to me, to your wife! Clear your conscience! No, don't touch me! Say nothing; I dare not hear anything. Oh, how awful! I want to get away from here. I want to go to Aunt Do. Or rather to the home for battered wives! Take me there, Watson, please! It would be the end of our happiness and the reward for my boundless love!"

The whole day was spent trying to calm Mrs Watson's agitated nerves. It was only towards nightfall that I succeeded in convincing her that I had been summoned to the police as a witness, not as an accused, but then I succeeded so completely that at the moment of parting, she embraced me with the words: "Go, my dearly beloved, go and fight chivalrously for your friend! Strike down his false detractors! He was a great man and a good man, an honour to old England. Around such always, envy spins its web. Tear them asunder, and come back to receive the reward of victory from your mate's hand!"

At Scotland Yard, I was ushered into the magistrate's office, where I already found Lord Redmooreland, Mr Stripers, Inspector Gregson, and the bankers Errand and Grill; the magistrate himself had not yet appeared. When I saluted, his Lordship turned away with an angry growl; Mr Stripers bowed coldly, as did the bankers. Only Mr Gregson said confidentially: "Damned unpleasant business, this, doctor. Who could have thought such a thing? I shall miss him, sir; sharp head, but damned haughty".

Now, Holmes was brought in between two officers. He was as broken and absent-minded as on the evening of the sixteenth when I visited him. When I offered him my hand, he smiled wanly and said:

"Different from the dream of Bandalore! I have brought so many here, and now I am here myself. The irony of fate, Watson! You realise I'm innocent, right? But what does it matter? My power is gone, my spirit has departed since I saw myself. My time is short; I've had orders, two orders, Doctor. What does it matter if I die in a cell or my bed in Baker Street?"

The judge entered, and the examination began. His honour stated the facts concerning the Harun al Rashid manuscript in a few words and otherwise referred to Mr Stripers, who gave a clear and detailed account of the taking of the deposit, substantially in accordance with the newspapers' account. Mr Errand was the official who released the deposit; he and Mr Grill, his supervisor, were very familiar with the appearance of Sherlock Holmes and testified that he was the one who deposited and took the deposit. Nor did my testimony improve my friend's position, for I must confess that on Saturday, 29 August, in a nervous and anxious state, he collected from me the certificate of deposit which he had left in my custody the day before.

"Mr Holmes," said the judge, "as you hear, the evidence is strongly against you. What have you to say in your defence?"

"Nothing but that I am innocent," replied my friend dully. "I never took the deposit out of the bank, and Mr Watson is mistaken; I never took the receipt from him."

"Holmes, you should realise that this system of absolute denial of established facts is meaningless. Would it not be better to make a sincere confession? The favours you have done to justice would then be credited to you. Where have you put the parchment?"

"Yes, you scoundrel, what have you done with the parchment?" sounded the angry growl of his Lordship.

"No insulting words, Your Honour," the judge admonished. "Even the accused is under the protection of the law. Mr Holmes, you who have sorted out so many tangled webs, sort out your own."

Holmes shook his head gloomily and indifferently.

"I can't do it, sir. My head is confused, my faculties are gone. I am innocent, a victim of a strange chain of circumstances."

"Can you deny the truth of the testimony of your friend Dr Watson, Mr Grill and Mr Errand?"

"I deny nothing. Everything is a riddle to me. Everything else is indifferent to me, sir."

"Then I fear the worst for you, and your obstinacy does not improve your case. Gentlemen, the hearing is closed for the day. Officers, take away..."

He didn't have time to finish the sentence; a porter came in and hurriedly handed him a couple of business cards; after reading the names on them, he told the messenger:

"Let the gentlemen come in, and you, Holmes, stay while we hear what they have to say."

The judge bowed reverently as the two gentlemen entered. In one, I recognised Colonel Glower, and in the other, no less a person than the Foreign Secretary of England.

The latter spoke: "Your Honour, the newspapers have brought to our notice the misfortune of Mr Holmes, and my debt of gratitude to him for efficient and discreet assistance on several important occasions has induced me to hasten here to give him all the assistance I can. My friend, Colonel Glower, has accompanied me for the same purpose."

"Your Honour's intervention is as commendable as it is much needed," said the judge politely. "What information can you provide?"

"If I understand the newspaper reports correctly, Mr Holmes is accused of having taken a deposit belonging to Lord Redmooreland from the Bank of England on the morning of Saturday, 29 August?"

"Quite right, Your Honour."

"Can you give the exact time when this would have happened?"

Mr Errand knew it. "It was between eleven and twelve. I had lunch between twelve and one, and I remember very well that the deposit was taken before but not very far before lunch." Mr Grill confirmed his colleague's statement.

I was also asked about the time I handed over the certificate of deposit. My reception time is half past ten to one; it had just begun when Mr. Holmes arrived. He had, therefore, left and taken the certificate with him sometime between half past ten and a quarter to eleven.

"It appears, then," said the Minister, "that we can establish that Mr Holmes's visit to the doctor and the bank took place between half-past ten and twelve o'clock on Saturday the 29th. I am glad to be able to state here that from 10.45 to 12.15 on the same day, Mr. Holmes was in my study for a consultation on the affairs of a high-ranking foreign person. Mr Glower was present and can attest to the truth of this, as can my Cabinet Secretary and the Ministry's caretaker. I am quite sure of the dates, as before the meeting with Mr Holmes, I had a consultation with the Spanish Ambassador and, afterwards, with the Council of Ministers."

Holmes raised his head. "That's right, your honour. I remember it now; I had quite forgotten it. My poor brain is in such a state."

"An alibi!" Gregson exclaimed.

"Gentlemen," said the judge, "this is very surprising and very puzzling. How am I to understand this? Mr. Errand and Mr. Grill have seen Holmes in the bank at eleven or twelve o'clock, but your Lordship and Colonel Glower have been conferring with him in the ministerial hotel at the same time. This is beyond my comprehension."

It was beyond our comprehension. If only Sherlock Holmes had been himself, how easily he would have solved the whole thing. But he wasn't. He had seen his other self and was now just a shadow of his former self.

A noise of hurried footsteps from the corridor interrupted the tense silence that had fallen in the room. A door opened, and a weasel-like face looked in.

"Mr Magistrate," the thin-faced man exclaimed hurriedly but suddenly stopped. With a look of surprise, he stood speechless and motionless on the threshold, staring at my friend Holmes.

"What do you want, Lestrade?" the judge asked impatiently.

"Good God!" exclaimed the famous detective Lestrade - for the man in the doorway was he. "Am I mad, or what is the matter? Sherlock Holmes here!"

The judge became even more irritated. "You are behaving strangely, Lestrade, your behaviour astonishes me. State what you have to say and then leave."

But Lestrade did not have an ear for his superior's words.

"Sherlock Holmes here! And I left him a moment ago down in the guardroom!"

"Are you drunk in the middle of the morning, sir?"

"No, indeed not, Your Honour. I have hardly eaten or drunk in 18 hours."

"Then explain what's going on."

"That is why I have come here, Your Honour, straight from the train without taking a bite to eat or tasting a drop. I have the honour to inform you that I have succeeded in arresting the criminal Sherlock Holmes."

"Arrest Sherlock Holmes? He's sitting right here."

Lestrade shook his head. "I don't understand a word of this, but as I live and breathe, I arrested Sherlock Holmes last night in Southampton."

"There must be some strange misunderstanding," said the judge thoughtfully. "Lestrade, make your report."

The detective said: "When the report of Holmes' crime came in at noon on 1 September, it struck me at once what a service to justice and what an honour to myself it would be if I succeeded in apprehending the criminal. I took it for granted that he had not remained at his residence, hardly in London. However, I was at a loss. I had set my spies in motion, and their information was conflicting; one had seen him, though disguised, in Brixton Road, another at the same time in the neighbourhood of London Bridge; a third had seen him buying a ticket for Dover. The last seemed most likely; I decided to follow that lead.

No Sherlock Holmes had travelled by steamer from Dover, and no one was in town. I had to turn back after a fruitless search. Then I had an inspiration from heaven, disembarked at Ashford and made my enquiries. They were crowned with success. A person who must be Holmes had changed trains at Ashford and travelled to Hastings.

I do not want to tire Mr Judge with the details of my reconnaissance. Holmes proved to be a cunning fox, never following his path straight ahead but constantly veering off into side tracks, but I never lost him. And last night, I caught him in Southampton just as he was transferring his suitcase to an Atlantic steamer. I brought him here on the early morning train and have him under surveillance down there."

"Down there, sir? He's sitting here," said the judge.

Lestrade shook his head. "If I understand…"

His Honour the Minister came to the aid of the confused justice. "Wouldn't it be best to let Mr Lestrade bring his prisoner here?"

The judge's face brightened. "You are right, your honour, right as always. Lestrade, fetch the fellow!"

The few minutes the inspector was gone felt like an eternity of intense tension. At last, the door opened, and all of us' eyes locked with a silly stare. Holmes rose hastily to his feet and exclaimed in horror, "My other self! What is the meaning of this?"

Inside the room, two identical copies of Sherlock Holmes stood opposite each other, identical in every detail of facial features, physique, and movements—an unprecedented miracle. Our eyes wandered from one to the other, uncertain, amazed, and wondering.

"Who are you?" the judge finally asked the latest arrival.

"Sherlock Holmes is my name; I'm sure it's familiar to you, Mr Magistrate," replied the interviewee, unperturbed.

"Is your name Sherlock Holmes?" repeated the representative of justice.

"Without a doubt, sir."

The judge turned to the other. "But who are you?"

My friend shrugged. "Your Honour, you have just established that I am Sherlock Holmes."

The judge turned back to the newcomer.

"So you are Sherlock Holmes?"

"I told you that, sir."

"Then who is the other one?"

"How should I know? Please ask him."

"What is your profession?"

"Private investigator with a certain reputation."

"Your home address?"

"221B Baker Street."

"Can you describe the property?"

"Of course. The apartment consists of a large reception room and two smaller ones, one of which was previously occupied by my friend Dr Watson. The reception room has a slightly worn carpet with some burnt holes - I have the habit of tapping my pipe against the edge of the table, which also bears the marks of that - of the four armchairs, one is a little wobbly on the right front leg -"

"That will do, sir." The judge shook his head helplessly. But I could no longer keep quiet. "That man over there is not Sherlock Holmes; his hands are clean, but my friend's fingers are stained from handling chemicals."

Even Mr Gregson exclaimed: "The more I look at the man, the more certain I am that he is not Sherlock Holmes."

Lestrade cast an angry glance at his colleague. "You're just saying that out of jealousy because it was me and not you who managed to catch him."

"Shut up, Lestrade, or I'll have you thrown out," thundered the judge, who found an opportune moment to vent the irritation that the situation had caused him.

Again, the Minister intervened. "Will you allow me, Your Honour, to ask the man a few questions?"

"More than happy to, Your Honour."

The Minister turned to the last person to arrive:

"Where were you on the morning of Saturday the twenty-ninth?"

"Where was I? In several places. Unfortunately, my profession does not allow me to sit in my county seat all the time."

"Were you with me?"

"Yes, that was me, sir."

"Why didn't you say so right away?"

"I assumed that for your own sake, you were not keen to proclaim it from the rooftops. One prefers to wash one's dirty laundry indoors."

"In whose company did you come to me?"

"My profession requires me to avoid all indiscretions. Half of England would blush with shame if I started gossiping out of school."

"Do you remember what we talked about?"

"Very well."

"How much was the ransom?"

"The ransom? I've actually forgotten. I have so much on my mind, sir. Was it five pounds or just three shillings or half a million? It was something like that."

"What would the man from Aldershot do?"

"Look here, sir. You are neither a judge nor a detective, I see; you are too clever for that. Well, sir, you have put me on the spot, and I am not a man who likes to make trouble and cause people unnecessary inconvenience - after all, meandering only serves to buy a few more months of confinement. Well, gentlemen, I'll press the truth, as the farmer said when he milked the ox: there's Sherlock Holmes and here's Jo Stangerton, formerly the leading actor of Levi's and Starke's travelling theatre company, now a bit of everything, as the case may be, king when I've got five shillings in my pocket, fool when my purse is empty."

A sudden light went on for the judge.

"Jo Stangerton! You have used your resemblance to Mr Holmes to play his part and usurp the parchment?"

"You hit the nail on the head, sir! I'm surprised you could figure it out!"

"It was to him that I left the deposit slip!" I exclaimed.

"Watson! It was no second sight! It was a flesh and blood creature I saw," Holmes whispered to me, his face beaming with ecstatic joy.

"I've caught the thief anyway!" Lestrade triumphed.

"But you were deceived when you thought you were following Mr Holmes' trail," Gregson interjected.

"Scoundrel, where is my parchment?" The Lord's growl cut through the murmur.

Stangerton turned to the latter with a polite bow: "I understand you are Lord Redmooreland. I regret that I cannot be of service with that information. You see, I am just a simple labourer who delivers the product to the employer. He handles the distribution."

"Who is this?" the judge asked.

"A good master, sir, and one who has far too long arms for me to dare to compromise him; I would rather take three years' hard labour."

"Where has the parchment gone?"

"Only he knows that. I followed orders and handed it to one of his helpers, who waited outside the bank and made the agreed sign. Since then, I have seen neither the parcel nor the helper."

It is unnecessary to describe the further course of the search. The result is shown in the following extract from the London newspaper:

"Sensational!

Innocence always triumphs!

Mr Sherlock Holmes' vindication.

A scam story without equal!!!

We are glad to inform our readers that the unpleasant affair in which our famous - we may well say world-famous - private detective, Mr Sherlock Holmes, has been involved has been cleared up in a manner which has fully proved his innocence and incorruptibility. Every reasonable man must also have realised beforehand that a crime committed by this man, so revered and unforgettable in the annals of English justice, must have been an anomaly, not to say an impossibility. Nor have we believed, even for a moment, in the absurdity of the rumour which was damaging to him.

Taking advantage of an astonishing external resemblance to Mr. Holmes, further enhanced by an exceptional capacity for mimicry, a disgraced former actor, Jo Stangerton, who has had several brushes with the law in America and Ireland, has succeeded in obtaining the aforementioned certificate of deposit and appropriating the precious manuscript deposited by Lord R. in the Bank of England. The honour of having apprehended the villain belongs to our distinguished detective, Mr. Lestrade, at present the foremost of his profession within the borders of England.

It is rumoured that the perpetrator of the crime is a certain learned gentleman whose account with justice is as great as it is unsettled but whose name we do not wish to mention for reasons of freedom of the press.

The stolen object has not been recovered; the owner, Lord R., is thus suffering a considerable and regrettable loss."

My friend Mr Holmes thus received the redress he had a right to expect. However, the events had so affected his nerves that he was obliged to give up work for a month and rest in Nice.

When he returned from there, healthy and strong, he said to me:

"Actually, I am grateful to that Jo Stangerton. He has forever freed me from the superstitious belief in second sight, which rode me like a nightmare and threatened to choke me. But in any case, Watson, the story of Harun al Rashid's parchment will be one of the strangest you have ever recorded. People will hardly believe it to be true."

One day in October, Holmes showed me two letters. One contained only the following lines:

"Mr Holmes! You are a man of honour! I want to tell you my opinion. Come visit Burgham Castle and see my museum and its precious treasure: Harun al Rashid's parchment!

Arthur, Lord Redmooreland."

The content of this was further explained by the second letter. It read:

"Lord Redmooreland! Honourable sir!

You replied rudely to my letter in April, yes rudely is exactly the right word. But if you thought you could make fun of me, sir, you thought wrong. I have no ancestry, sir - my grandfather came to this country as a shirtless beggar - but I am a gentleman, sir, a free American citizen, and have money enough to buy one of your English counties. What I set my mind to do, I am doing, and I had set my mind to get hold of your old parchment - Stratch would not make triumph smile in my face. If I could not buy your parchment, I could borrow it. I have done so; a friend of mine has arranged it through a friend and friends of a friend. It costs money, but Stratch will pay for it. Now, the parchment is being returned with thanks for the loan. Professor Ward has wrapped it so that it is undamaged - he understands such things better than you or I. I hope you're not angry with me for the little joke I played on you. You see, it doesn't pay to try to fool a Yankee gentleman.

Can you imagine how bright blue-green Stratch turned when I showed him the parchment, and the professor explained that it was genuine? To this day, my stomach aches from laughing at it.

Your affectionate

D. Josef Curvill

P.S. As rent for the parchment, I have sent to your address a cask of 'Curvill's original best brown stout' and recommend myself to your favourable consideration for future use."

"Watson," said Holmes, after I had returned the letters to him, "I think we have been involved in a new version of Shakespeare's comedy: 'All's well that ends well.'"

"I think so, too," I said aloud. Inside, I added: "And I wish I could play the lead in a new version of 'The Taming of the Shrew.'"

6. MOLLY

L**ETTER** from Dr Watson to Sture Stig.

Dear Mr. Stig!

I sit down to write to you. Why I do it, I do not understand. I'm really not a fan of scribbling things down on paper; most of the time, it just turns into nonsense.

So why am I writing? Perhaps it is because of the rain, which pours down and prevents a person from looking outside the door, let alone a patient from visiting my waiting room - unless it was someone who was already dying.

Or do I see you as Benjamin Franklin's literally brilliant invention personified? Are you my lightning rod? Maybe I am. At least I needed one here. After all, the air is charged with electricity, and there's been a lot of crackling and sparking in both the bedroom and the dining room all morning. The crackling was undeniably reminiscent of Mrs Watson's voice, and the sparks came from her beautiful, gentle eyes. 'She's gone to Auntie Do for the moment, just for the moment, Mr Stig.

Or am I writing to you out of sympathy? Perhaps I am. Our acquaintance was fleeting, but you have shown that you understand and appreciate me, Mr. Stig, and there is no surer basis for sympathy and friendship than admiration. Love is a firework, Mr Stig, suns and stars that go out, and then everything gets twice as dark. And friendship? You meet your closest comrade from Eton and Oxford, you are overjoyed, you let your soul take a refreshing dip in the sea of happy school memories, and you say: "Old boy, you and I shall always be of one heart and soul as of old", and then you hear that he is applying for the same post as you, or that he has won the lottery where you only got a draw, or he pats you on the shoulder very kindly and says: "Watson, you old man of honour, lend me £50!" - and that's the end of the friendship and the bosom friend! But admiration, Mr Stig, binds people together like handcuffs. You admire me, therefore I like you and will do so as long as your feelings for me remain unchanged.

What should I actually write to you about? Parliament is on holiday - you know that; it is raining - it has all summer. Mr Galton, the stockbroker, has bought the Duke of Alberville's picture gallery, and Sir Joshua Lipton is thinking of a new America's Cup race - the newspapers have told you all that. The newspapers are the cabbage worms in the garden of news; they eat up everything that would serve to nourish and profit others.

But it is true, I have one piece of news: Count Valricco is dead, the former diplomat, you know. He died last Thursday of indigestion after a dinner at the German Consul's house. The latter patriotic gentleman had decorated his table with German flags and German dishes. The Count was a spoilt man and a sophisticated gourmé: the roast beef and sauerkraut were too much for him. He literally succumbed and gave his life for the honour of Germany.

I had the honour of knowing the Count; the acquaintance was established in a rather peculiar way - Sherlock Holmes, of course, was the connecting link. It's quite a story. You like them, don't you? I might as well tell it to you as fill twenty pages with talk without content or meaning. So listen, Mr. Stig! I will tell you, after first assuring you that I will always remain your devotee.

Watson.

I have been criticised for monotony. They say I always begin my stories in the same way, always in the same situation: Sherlock Holmes at the table in the reception room, rubbing his violin or tapping his pipe against the edge of the table, myself half-asleep, looking through a newspaper or a book. It is my pleasure to begin this story truthfully in a very different way. It was my friend Holmes who was reading the paper, and I was pacing up and down the room with my hands behind my back, when a rustle of silk was heard outside the door, and a couple of ladies entered.

"It was as if the dark room had suddenly been filled with a radiant flood of sun and light." I wish I could apply this poetic phrase to our situation, which I read the other day in a novel. But unfortunately that would be to distort the truth. The room did not get any brighter, quite the opposite. I have every respect for ladies and a distinct fear of offending them - Mrs. Watson has taught me that - but the truth above all, and this is the truth, is that the two ladies did not possess to

          FRANS OSKAR WÅGMAN

any great extent the all-pervading glow of youth, beauty or pleasure.

The first entrant was black, this was the general impression of her; the dress was of stiff black silk, the darkness of which was only broken by a long heavy gold chain and a small, very small jewelled brooch; hair, eyes, and eyebrows were jet black, and the complexion, if not exactly of the same colour, was unusually dark - like that of a Portuguese, I should say, though I have never seen a Portuguese lady; black also was the heavy shading of her upper lip, especially near the corners of her mouth. She had a sharply cut face, with a thin nose and small mouth, and a figure of medium height, which averted all suspicion of fondness for the pleasures of an opulent table, the bearing of a lady-in-waiting at the queen's grand reception, and the countenance of a general on a day of battle. I may add that the lady has long since seen both her first and second springs disappear into the sea of the past, though she has not yet lost any of the vigour and energy of middle age; I estimated her age at a glance at about 50.

Her companion had probably seen the light of day at about the same time, though over her person, there rested what I would call a shadow of youth, for there was certainly something ghostly in it. She was tall, and had a figure almost too voluptuous; her face, from which shone a pair of large aqua-blue eyes, looking out into the world with a surprised expression, was surrounded by flaxen hair, done up in a girlish manner. The same features were to be found in the clothes, with their bright colours in shades of blue and grey, and in the manner of movement, where, however, it was essentially counteracted by an innate slowness.

The lady in black spoke up: "We are looking for Mr Holmes."

"That's me," he replied, bowing slightly, "and this is my trusted friend and assistant, Dr Watson."

"You are of course surprised to see us here, Mr Holmes, but you may be sure that we have not taken such a step without mature consideration and much self-conquest."

"No, we don't," confirmed the younger lady.

"Oh, why?"

"Would that surprise you, Mr Holmes?" said the black-clad one. "We are ladies, and you are a bachelor."

"Very well put, Ciss," agreed the other lady.

My friend smiled. "Oh, as for that, you may depend upon it that I have received visits from ladies here at all hours of the day."

The black-clad woman straightened up in all her dignity.

"Verily, my lord, this is language which I did not expect from you, and which I cannot allow in my presence."

"No, we can't, Ciss," repeated the echo in grey and blue. "It is not a language for younger ladies' ears."

"But you are excused, sir," admitted the black-clad good-hearted woman. "Your profession brings you into contact only with the lower, uneducated, sinful strata of society."

My friend smiled again; he obviously found pleasure in the behaviour of the two ladies.

"On this chair, which I most humbly request you to occupy, sat yesterday the Marquise of Westonbridge, and on this, which I have the honour to offer to the young lady, your companion, His Royal Highness Prince George of Slavonia rested for more than an hour less than eight days ago."

The ladies looked at my friend with narrowed eyes; the circumstances he had mentioned made him grow in their judgement into a greatness which they found difficult to meet. They also sat down with reverence as if they had been offered a seat on the throne at the queen's side, and the one dressed in black said in an apologetic tone:

"Excuse me, sir! Of course I had not the slightest intention of offending so remarkable a person as yourself. My feminine delicacy, my natural modesty, heightened by a refined education, sir, prompted me to say those hasty words."

"They were hasty, Ciss, but easy to explain; you are so delicate and so modest," the echoes said.

"You didn't know who I was either," the woman in black continued, trying to exonerate my friend in his own eyes. "You probably don't know me."

"I'm afraid I don't have the honour."

"I am otherwise fortunate to be familiar, and I can happily say familiar..."

"You can, dear Ciss! Confidence is the right word."

"By her grace, Lady Rivers, the sweet Emily Rivers, by Miss Flora Curnershop, a sister of the Lord Chancellor's wife, by the Countess of Dumbarstone, who on my fifth ..., on my birthday, gave me this brooch 'in memory of a grateful former pupil,' as it said on the cover in which the brooch was enclosed. They have all been my pupils, and I have had the good fortune and honour to inculcate in them the high learning, the fine manners, and the noble principles which give them such a prominent place in the distinguished circles in which they move. For I am Miss Ingrahm, the owner and director of the celebrated educational establishment for young ladies of quality, called 'Ingrahm's Institute for Higher Education and the Art of Living,' of which you have doubtless heard."

"Unfortunately, not."

"Is that possible? Well, London is so big, and of course, you have other interests than education." Continuing the introduction, she pointed to her companion: "This is Miss Sladd, my assistant, friend and first teacher of French and Italian."

Miss Sladd smiled a seductive, youthful smile, and my friend bowed.

"Perhaps now I will know the reason for your honourable visit, Miss Ingrahm."

"Mr Holmes! After what you have now learnt about me, you should understand that only the most pressing necessity, only the most threatening circumstances could have induced me to take the step I have taken of coming to see you here."

"You had to do it, Cissy; you had no other choice," Miss Sladd encouraged her friend.

"Please tell us about these circumstances and do so as clearly and briefly as possible," Mr Holmes said.

The invitation did not go down particularly well.

"I teach English literature and English language at my institute, and always correct my pupils' written work in these subjects myself. I, therefore, consider myself a master of my expressive mother tongue with all its infinite possibilities. When I was young, I wrote a short story and sent it to the 'Woman's Gazette'; the editors sent it back saying that 'the world was not yet ripe for such a work.'"

"It was too profound! What thoughts and what style!" exclaimed Miss Sladd.

My friend's patience was beginning to wear thin; it had been unusually resilient, but even the strongest rope breaks under too much strain.

"Please get to the point, Miss. The minutes are running out fast, and my time is precious and strictly occupied. What are the threatening circumstances to which you referred?"

"Mr Holmes! Perhaps a lady of my education and connections could claim more respectful treatment, but you are right, time is short and precious."

"Oh yes," sighed Miss Sladd, "time flies."

"I have been in a deadly state of anxiety and worry for three days, and the reason is - Val, should I really tell?"

Val, that is to say, Miss Valentine Sladd, to whom this question of conscience was addressed, shook her bright head, but assumed a determined air.

"It is unpleasant, dear Ciss, most unpleasant, but it cannot be avoided. You must speak, must do violence to your feelings and speak. That is why we have come here."

Val's determination clearly infected her friend Cissy.

"Well, sir, listen! The fact is that a man has tried to enter the restricted area of the Ingrahm Institute!"

Miss Ingrahm said this in a tone as if she expected that the fact stated would make my friend Holmes jump out of his chair, or at least utter a loud cry of astonishment. Neither, however, was the case; with a calmness that almost contained a touch of irony, he merely asked:

"Well, and then?"

"And then? I don't know whether you understood my words, Mr Holmes. I said that a man had tried to get into Ingrahm's Institute, an institution devoted to education and female purity. A man, Mr Holmes!"

"Think about it, a man!" repeated the echo.

My friend was at pains to betray the feelings which this remark aroused in him - he knew from recent experience Miss Ingrahm's way of 'mastering the language with all its possibilities'. He stifled his smile and said briefly:

"Please give all the details from the beginning."

Miss Ingrahm began:

"Ingrahm's Institute is situated in Glover Street, as you know, a fashionable, quiet, still street; on the other side is Primrose Park, an oasis in the noisy desert of London - the picture, Mr Holmes, is perhaps not very accurate, but very expressive. The institute has a garden of 1,283 square metres, adorned with two chestnut trees, a walnut tree and countless shrubs. Here, the pupils of the Institute have the privilege of daily walks in the fresh air, enjoying the beauty and innocence of nature, and, in the younger years, full liberty to play and frolic, under the competent supervision, of course, of a teacher, and with careful regard to what care for the preservation of dress and good behaviour may require. I need not mention that the garden is surrounded by a high and close iron fence, to whose only gate I myself keep the key.

A young girl, Deborah Westrow, is employed at the Institute as an assistant teacher of the youngest children. Her father was a City businessman and was considered wealthy; on that basis I was able to accept Debora as a pupil in my institution, even though she was not really from a good family, but I have bitterly regretted this departure from my principles. Just as Deb was finishing her education, her father died and - can you imagine? - turned out to be completely penniless. His wealth had been but a shimmering soap bubble in the business world's sky. I lost three pounds six shillings in pure money by his bankruptcy, but still my good heart prevailed over my reason, and I let Deb stay at the Institute as an assistant teacher; I had not the heart to throw her out on the street. I even gave her a salary, a pound and three shillings a quarter, plus the benefits of food at the children's table, free laundry, and the prospects of employment at the Ingrahm Institute. But do you think she showed any particular gratitude? Even as a pupil, she caused me trouble by her thoughtless, I would almost say frivolous, manner and behaviour. She would not walk but run; she rejected the good food of the Institute, gave our excellent tea the vulgar epithet of 'black,' and showed a good deal of similar ill behaviour; once, I even caught her seducing some other girls into playing blind man's buff. They sat on each other's lap! I hoped that the death of her father would steady her character and poverty would humble her mind, and indeed, this seemed to be the case, for a year now, she has been more thoughtful and submissive than before. But then suddenly came the shock.

It was Monday; I was sitting alone in the teachers' room correcting papers - the teachers had lessons. Then little Alice Drebber comes in breathless and says: 'Miss Ingrahm, Deborah is in the garden...' Alice is a pretty girl, I should almost say my favourite, if my duties as an educator allowed me to deviate one millimetre from the narrow path of impartiality; she is only eleven years old, but she has a remarkable acuteness of vision and a love of truth without equal; everything she discovers of less good qualities in her peers she reports conscientiously and at once to me. You may judge, however, Mr Holmes, of the earnestness with which I embrace my position as an educator, when, in spite of my fondness for little

Alice, I did not overlook her disrespectful mention of a teacher. 'Alice, my child,' said I, 'a pupil does not say Deborah, but Miss Westrow, or at least Miss Deborah. But what was it you wanted to say, dear?' I saw by the child's eyes that she had something interesting to tell me; they shone with eagerness and pleasure.

'Miss Deb' - the child could not bring herself to associate anything other than the abbreviation with the title Miss - 'Miss Deb is standing by the fence in the garden talking to a man.'

My pen made a large red stain in my notebook; for a pupil, such a mistake could not have been made with less than 300 penal verses from Milton or a couple or three chapters from the Bible; you can judge from this circumstance the anxiety that seized me. A man at the fence of our garden! A member of the Institute's teaching staff talking to a man who, moreover, is not the father, brother or guardian of any of the pupils! If he had been, he would have turned to me.

I jumped up from my chair and hurried down to the garden. I wanted to investigate the matter myself and avert the scandal. I found Deborah sitting on a bench under the walnut tree; little Molly Nessle, the four-year-old she had been put in charge of, was playing with the sand on the path at her feet. There was no sign of any man.

I made a serious enquiry of Debora, a very serious enquiry. She admitted that she had spoken to the man through the fence; he had called out to her and asked her the name of the park; she had told him, and he had thanked her; that was all. She seemed to have no idea that she had done anything wrong or inappropriate. I took the time to judge for myself of her offence and the punishment that should follow, and gave her some cordial but severe admonitions. As, however, I had little confidence in either Deborah's record or character, I urged little Alice to keep her eyes open, especially when Deborah was in the garden.

The need for my precautions would soon become apparent. Already on Wednesday, Alice reported that the man was standing by the fence, and Deborah was talking to him.

I did not rush downstairs as I had done last time; I wanted to catch the culprit red-handed, so I proceeded cautiously, took the kitchen stairs, and crept through the bushes to the place of the meeting. My footsteps, however, must have been heard on the sandy path, for when I caught sight of the place, I saw the man hurry away and disappear into the leafy plantations of the park. But Deborah was still standing by the fence, holding little Molly. She blushed and paled by turns; she knew her judgement. I passed it on to her with all the indignation of my wounded feelings of virtue and modesty. Within two days she must leave the institute, and until she left it forever, not set foot outside the door of the house.

You think, Mr Holmes, that she was depressed and devastated? No, Mr Holmes. Her heart, as well as her brow, was stone; she was neither moved nor ashamed. She had done nothing wrong; she had hardly said five words to the man; he had eyes only for Molly, he was so fond of little children. Who he was, she did not know, hardly what he looked like; young he was, she must admit, and handsome - perhaps, but too feminine to be to her taste; she liked manliness in a man.

That's what she said to me, Cecilia Ingrahm! My cheeks were flushed with embarrassment; I could not give her the rebuke she deserved. Emboldened by my silence, she explained that no harm had been done, nothing untoward had happened, when she was suddenly interrupted by an unexpected voice:

"Didn't I see him reach through the fence, grab Molly under the chin and pat her on the cheek!"

It was little Alice who had followed me unseen and now came to my aid so unexpectedly.

"Ah, you're the little spy! I should have guessed you had a hand in it," said Deborah contemptuously. "Well, if he stroked Molly's cheek, what of it?"

"He was petting the baby, but he meant the nurse. Have you ever heard that expression before?" Alice replied triumphantly.

Alice Drebber was an unusually gifted, developed and perceptive child. She expressed exactly the same thought that was stirring within me. But where had she seen these dark sides of human nature, these moral aberrations that she seemed to know so well? In the pure, ideal atmosphere of the Ingrahm Institute? It was impossible, and yet she had spent her life there since she was five years old. And where had she learnt that saying, so apt as the expressions of the lower classes always are according to the latest findings of science, yet so vulgar? It was a mystery to me. But at least Alice Drebber was a lovable, richly gifted and truth-loving child, and the circumstances did not allow for deeper thoughts or questions. Deborah's last statement expressed such inward depravity and contempt for virtue and decency that I would have humiliated myself in my own eyes if I had allowed her to stay overnight in my house. She had to leave, not after two days, but after two hours. Was she horrified, abandoned and humbled, Mr Holmes? No, she was not. 'Better anywhere, even in the street, than here,' said the impudent creature. Thinking back on her words and behaviour, my nerves still tremble like taut strings.

"Calm down, dear Cissy, calm down by all means! Remember that you are so sensitive and fragile!" Miss Sladd admonished sympathetically.

"Is that all? Is this what you have come to see me about, Miss Ingrahm?" Sherlock Holmes said, his patience running out. The Black Miss, however, did not seem to foresee the possibility of such a thing, but went on:

"Everything? Oh, no, Mr Holmes, the worst, the awful, the terrible remains. But I am really too upset by the memory of Deb's behaviour to go on. Val, my friend, won't you tell Mr Holmes about Thursday night's events? You are the best person to do so, my dear Val, for you were an eye-witness."

"Of course, I do, my dear Ciss, I'll do anything for you, and I'll tell you all about it as best I can, but

　　　　　FRANS OSKAR WÅGMAN

you'll have to forgive me, Mr Holmes, for I haven't my honourable friend's rhetorical powers at all."

As Mr Holmes declared himself perfectly satisfied without having to enjoy her precious flow of words, Miss Sladd spoke up.

"I am a coward, I know, and am usually very much afraid to go out as soon as it is dark; I am such a sensitive person, Mr Holmes. But last night, I departed from my habit and went out into the garden after the sun had long since set. The stars of the sky were glittering in the firmament like a huge jewel of diamonds. But it was not this that drew me out, but something I hate to mention. You know what it was, dear, understanding Cissy."

"I know that," she replied, more briefly than an understanding friend should.

"You want to know everything, every detail, you have said, Mr Holmes. I may have to reveal even this to you, even if it tears open deep wounds in your heart."

"I don't think it's necessary at all," the friend interjected rather unkindly.

"If it's not necessary to explain the matter, you can skip it, Miss Sladd," added Holmes.

"I think it's necessary, Cissy, it's part of the business, Mr Holmes, or I might appear to you in quite the wrong light. A girl out in a garden after dark! What would you think of me? So listen, Mr Holmes, I want to show you my heartbreak. Thursday last week is the great day of the sorrow of my life; eight years ago that day, Captain Morton passed away from the earthly and the happiness that waited by my side; he was my fiancé, and died of cholera at Benares, but lived forever in the heart of his faithful Val, which shall never, never be given to any other man, even if a duke should ask for it."

"I don't think you'll be tempted, my dear," interposed Miss Cissy, who had her own special reasons for not feeling too much pity for her friend's bleeding heart. For she had reason, and good reason, to suppose that the love of the said Captain Morton, and possibly even of the captain himself, had never existed except in Miss Sladd's vivid imagination and love-thirsty soul. Miss Sladd pretended not to hear the sarcasm, but continued: "I went out into the garden; my feelings were too deeply agitated to remain indoors. Above me arched the blue starry sky, and in front of me lay the white facade of the house shrouded in semi-darkness, for a gas lantern from Gower Street cast a faint glow on it. A deep melancholy seized my spirit. My soul flew over land and sea to the pagodas and palm trees of Benares."

Holmes made an impatient movement. "That one is seven journeys worse than the other," he whispered to me, but aloud, he said: "Miss Sladd, I should be very grateful if you could make your visit to India as short as possible and return to London."

"I apologise, Mr Holmes. My emotions took over; it shall not happen again. A person of the stronger sex cannot, of course, understand what is stirring in the soul of a young woman. So, back to cold reality - the evening was indeed raw and cold. I lowered my eyes from the sky, when I saw something that almost made my blood run cold. A little way up the wall of the house, I saw a dark shadow, which gradually took a firmer shape and showed me the image of a man - the slim figure of my unforgettable Morton, I thought. Was it his ghost come to earth in this way to express his appreciation of my faithful remembrance, or was it he in real form, and was the news of his death but a tale? What did I know? I approached the house and called out, 'Morton, is that you?' when, with a jump, the figure stood on the ground some distance from me, stared at me with a terrible look, and then disappeared into the garden as if swallowed up by the earth. It was not Morton, nor his ghost; it was a living creature, Mr Holmes, and a man who had climbed up the stone steps and tried to look in at a window."

Miss Ingrahm had recovered enough composure to take part in the discussion. "Footprints were clearly visible this morning in the soft earth beneath the window, and the marks of his feet on the projecting edge of the stone foot."

"Did you make any enquiries last night to find out if the man was hiding in the garden?"

"You forget, Mr Holmes, that in the Ingrahm Institute, there are only women. Would we go out looking for a man in the middle of the night?"

"Have you contacted the police, Miss Ingrahm?"

"The police? I would never do that. I asked on Monday for a constable to keep a lookout so that no one else would be allowed to stop at the fence, but the police said they had other things to do than guard young girls and old schoolmistresses."

"And what do you want me to do?" Holmes asked.

"You are going to save us from that man. Who is this man? What does he want? Is he a thief? Or a murderer?" Miss Ingrahm exclaimed.

"Or an arsonist?" Miss Val added.

Holmes sat thoughtfully back in his chair for a few minutes, before saying:

"Who is he? What does he want? Who can answer that - now? Perhaps the whole thing is a trifle, a little romance with Miss Debora; perhaps it has a much deeper meaning. Miss Ingrahm, the doctor and I will accompany you to the institute and investigate the circumstances."

Miss Cissy and Miss Val exchanged glances; I understood their meaning: "Can we let a man into the Institute's restricted area?" They both bowed their heads in deep resignation, which I interpreted as: "Fate is forcing us. We have no choice but to accept."

"You don't have to go into the house itself, do you, Mr Holmes?" Miss Ingrahm asked.

"Probably not."

"So be it. Necessity has no law, and no one shall have just cause to blame us."

So it was that half an hour later, my friend and I found ourselves on the sacred ground of the Ingrahm Institute. All the pupils and teachers except the headmistress and her dear Val were to remain confined to their respective classrooms at all times during the examination, which did not, however, prevent me, playing the part of an idle and rather uninterested extra, from catching glimpses of a number of girls' faces in the windows. Perhaps there were more loose ends in the admirable educational mechanism of the Ingrahm Institute than both the outside world and the headmistress realised.

Suddenly, Sherlock Holmes interrupted himself in the middle of his investigations. "Is there anyone who can give a description of the man who spoke to the teacher Debora?"

"That would be little Alice Drebber," replied Miss Ingrahm.

"Call her over!" my friend ordered shortly.

"But, Mr Holmes, think - a child - what is appropriate." The miss was almost offended.

My friend looked her sharply in the eye.

"Bring me the girl, Miss! It may be more important than you realise."

It is a great proof of my friend's personal influence that even Miss Ingrahm felt defeated and obeyed. When she went to fetch the girl, however, she said: "Remember, sir, that the child is quite unaccustomed to male company. She will be afraid of you! Speak kindly to her!"

After a few moments, she came back with Alice by the hand. I could now see that all the windows of the house were full of the faces of children and women, who, in their eagerness to see what was going on, had quite forgotten their former caution.

"My child, can you describe the man you saw talking to Miss Debora at the fence?"

Holmes had not had to soften his rough voice into a rather affected friendliness; Alice was neither frightened nor shy; on the contrary, her lively eyes burned with the bright lustre of curiosity and contented vanity - she knew that the situation would make her the heroine of the school for at least a week.

"Yes, I can, sir. He was not tall, but narrow in waist and had small hands and feet. He was young, hardly more than twenty years old, and had not a hair of beard about his mouth. He wore a blue jacket, a waistcoat and trousers of the same colour, a polka-dotted scarf tied in a curiously feminine way in a large bow, and on his head, he wore a floppy hat that covered his forehead down to his eyebrows."

Holmes looked at the little girl in amazement. "You certainly have eyes in your head and brains, too," he exclaimed with a hint of admiration. "Thank you, my child, for your very enlightening description!"

He turned around and was about to continue his investigations when he was stopped by Alice, who grabbed his coat collar.

"I have something else to tell you," she half-whispered in a confidential, secretive tone. "You are a policeman, a very remarkable policeman, sir? Listen: it wasn't a man; it was a woman in disguise."

Holmes shrugged. "Oh! How do you know that?"

"I saw her hands when she petted little Molly. No man in the world has hands like that. And her waist was just like a woman's - you know, men are built quite differently from women."

Sherlock Holmes gave me a meaning, half-humoured look which meant: "At the Ingrahm Institute there are, I believe, sources of knowledge which do not flow from the well-filtered waters of the Ingrahmian springs of virtue." He did not have time to express his opinion on this in words, however, for the two souls so intimately united, Miss Ciss and Miss Val, raised a common exclamation of surprise:

"A woman in disguise? Impossible!" And Miss Val, who had reaped a richer harvest of experience in the field of women's hearts than Miss Cissy, added: "Then what interest had Deborah in talking to the person through the fence?"

"Little Miss Alice is probably right: I am even inclined to say she is right," said my friend, "and I compliment her on a power of observation unusual for her age. She really is a little detective."

Alice blushed with pleasure, but Miss Ingrahm was not yet convinced. "For what purpose would a woman in disguise be sneaking around my institute?"

"That's just what we have to find out, and with your permission, Miss, I'd like to get on with it. From all appearances, the matter seems to involve something much more serious than a little flirtation with Deborah."

"Mr Holmes, you frighten me!" Miss Val exclaimed, while Miss Ingrahm, feeling her important duty as an educator, exclaimed: "What cynicism, Mr Holmes! Think of the innocent child present!"

My friend did not hear the reproach; he was already busy with his investigations. I need not describe these, but only mention the results, which my friend announced when, half an hour later, we were sitting under the walnut tree, Holmes and I on the bench, the two mistresses on chairs, at a respectful distance, of course. To her obvious disappointment, the little detective Alice had been sent back to her classroom, where she was no doubt entertaining peers and possibly even teachers with interesting tales from the outside world.

"Alice was right," my friend began his account, "the mysterious person is a woman in disguise. Besides the child's shrewd observation, this is proved by the footprints she left in the soft earth of the garden and on the projecting edge of the stone foot; when she undressed, she forgot to change her shoes; hers are a woman's, and, moreover, belong to a pair of the snuggest female feet you can see."

"Who is she? If you, Miss Ingrahm, had not chased Deborah away from the house, we might now have answers to this and other questions; now, you have made it impossible for me to give any definite information for the moment. There is only one clue to go by. I wondered how she could get into and so quickly leave this garden, surrounded as it is by a high iron fence with sharp spikes. She has swung herself over with a quick jump, using a couple of the protruding spikes for support - one of which has scratched her finger and bears a small bloodstain as evidence. But few, even skilful male athletes, would risk such a jump and succeed in doing it, still less an ordinary woman; only one accustomed to acrobatic exercises could venture it and succeed. I conclude, therefore, that the unknown should be sought in a circus or an athletic society."

"A circus lady, a female athlete here in our garden, in our sanctuary dedicated to purity and education! This is even worse than if it had been a man!" Miss Ingrahm exclaimed in horror.

Holmes did not mind the interruption. "What does she want? That is the next question. There can be no flirtation with Deborah, of course, now that the gender of the stranger has been revealed, and there is probably no other connection between the teacher and the stranger, for if there had been, the latter would certainly have found out that Deborah had left the institute and had nothing more to seek here. But she came in the evening after Deborah was already gone, and what is more, Miss Ingrahm, she intends to come back."

"Come back? I'm absolutely amazed," exclaimed Miss Ciss.

"Oh, I'm so upset," echoed Miss Val, "it's so mysterious and frightening but so exciting."

"You ask how I know this? Simply because last night she took a wax impression of the key to the front door, my magnifying glass shows me some small wax particles in the keyhole that cannot be explained in any other way."

"What does she want? You frighten me, Mr Holmes. Does she want to steal? Does she want to murder us?" Miss Ingrahm almost trembled in her chair.

"Is she leading a gang of thieves, maybe a murder gang?" the echo repeated.

"What does she want?" Holmes said thoughtfully. "That is the very heart of the mystery. Look here, Miss Ingrahm, who is that child Molly?"

"Why do you ask that?"

"Because all the signs point to little Molly having a central role in this mysterious story. The disguised woman appears at the fence only when Deborah is in the garden with the child; she takes an interest in Molly and caresses her; the window she climbs up to and tries to look through - she did just that, Miss Sladd, when you thought you recognised the ghost of the late Captain Morton, my investigations have confirmed it - that window is the very room where, among other pupils, little Molly sleeps the deep sleep of childhood. All the circumstances point to Molly and no one else; the child is, in a way, the centre of the adventure, with her undoubtedly lies the key to the solution of the riddle. Therefore, I have asked: who is Molly? and I repeat the question."

"Mr Holmes! Molly Nessle is an orphan left in my care."

"By whom?"

"As Director of this Institute, I have sacred duties, Mr. Holmes, and among these, one of the most important is discretion. My discretion is trusted and can be trusted, sir. I would rather be torn to pieces between wild horses than betray a trust reposed in me, and such a trust is the name of the person who entrusted my darling Molly to me."

Holmes rose from the bench. "Goodbye, Miss Ingrahm, goodbye, Miss Sladd!"

A double exclamation of surprise caused a chaffinch, which had just begun to sing the first notes of its song in the walnut tree, to fall silent and fly away.

"What are you going to do, sir?" Miss Cissy asked.

"Of course, go my way," replied Holmes sternly. "My involvement in this matter is at an end. Instead of helping me, you are putting up a wall in my way, Miss. Good day to you. But take my advice: sleep with one eye open for the next few nights."

"Oh, Ciss, don't let Mr Holmes go!" Miss Sladd pleaded. "Don't let him go! Think of the wax in the keyhole!"

"Do you think that this woman would dare to enter the sanctuary of the Institute?" Miss Ciss asked anxiously, "Into the house itself?"

"It seems that was her intention," said Holmes dryly.

"A burglar, then!" Miss Ingrahm shouted.

"A murderess perhaps!" replied the echo.

"An acrobat, a circus lady, a tightrope walker in the Ingrahm Institute! What a scandal! My reputation would be ruined. Mr Holmes, save us! I will tell you everything."

"You can do it with a clear conscience, Ciss," her friend assured her.

"Well, Mr Holmes, I'll tell you everything I know myself. It is really not much. Molly has been left to me by Count Valricco, the envoy of the Kingdom of Albania to our court."

My friend let out a low whistle; it was a sign of excited interest mixed with surprise.

"Count Valricco?" he repeated. "And what information did he give you about the child?"

"That it was an orphan; as a friend of the parents, he wanted to take care of the poor abandoned creature."

"Goodbye, Miss!" Holmes got up again.

"What do you mean, sir? Goodbye? Why do you say that?"

"Because I don't believe you. You know more about the child than you want to reveal to me, but I have no desire to play blind man's buff like Deborah."

"I swear, Mr Holmes, by all that is holy, I swear I know nothing more."

"You didn't ask the Count?"

"You don't ask people like an ambassador."

"I suppose you've been trying to get information from little Molly."

"I have, sir. I considered it my duty. How could I fulfil my important mission as the child's teacher without trying to explore her thoughts, habits, personality and memories? In education, it is fundamental to take into account the individual characteristics of children. I have tried to explore Molly but to no avail. She has no memories. She was so small when she came here, only two years old."

"Do you know if Count Valricco is in London?"

"He is not. Eight days ago, he sent me the tuition fee half a month in advance, because he was planning to go on holiday."

"Where?"

"He didn't mention that in the letter."

Sherlock Holmes began to walk up and down the garden path, deep in thought. All our eyes followed him with eager anticipation. Finally, he stopped and said:

"This is a mysterious, indeed a very mysterious affair, and the only person who could throw light on the matter, Count Valricco, is out of reach. Besides, we know nothing about his role in the whole thing. He could be a guardian angel or a devil. One thing is likely, however: someone is trying to get hold of this child, Molly, to keep her away from the Count's influence. This is a theory that fits in well with all the known facts."

"What do you say, Mr Holmes? Is someone going to kidnap the child? And from my house, from the Ingrahm Institute?"

"Oh, so horrible, yet so exciting!"

The different personalities of the two teachers were reflected in these exclamations.

My friend only answered Miss Cissy. "No doubt that's what they intend to do."

"But what should I do? What am I going to do?"

"Listen, Miss," said my friend seriously. "Probably this thing is of much greater importance and significance than we realise. I wouldlike to look deeper into it, to the bottom. I don't like to leave a job half done; I don't like to leave unknown, shadowy areas behind me. I would like to see the unknown woman face to face and talk to her for five minutes. That's why I want to help you, Miss Ingrahm. It is certain that the unknown woman, alone or with an accomplice, will attempt to kidnap the child one of these nights, perhaps even tonight. Therefore, when darkness falls, the doctor and I will present ourselves at your gate into Glower Street. You will let us into the house, and we will keep watch in the corridor leading to little Molly's room, and arrest the stranger when she comes."

Miss Ingrahm jumped up and stretched her hands to the sky. "Mr Holmes! What are you thinking of? You and the doctor in the house - and at night!"

Miss Val was as upset as her friend. "Mr Holmes! We are decent women!" Her eyes expressed such a sense of deeply offended decency that they almost filled with tears.

"What would the world say and think of me?" Miss Cissy continued. "And these young women entrusted in my care! I should die of shame. Mr Holmes, can't you and the doctor keep watch outside the house?"

"And freeze from damp and cold and risk being discovered prematurely? No thanks, Miss Ingrahm."

"But perhaps the stranger intends to get in through the window of Molly's room. That's where she made her observations last night, isn't it?" objected Miss Sladd.

"Do you usually take an impression of the door lock when you intend to get in through the window?" my friend asked dryly.

"It's impossible, simply impossible, sir," explained Miss Ingrahm.

"Absolutely impossible," confirmed Ms Sladd.

"I could never look my innocent girls in the eye again."

"You could never do that, Ciss; you're so sensitive."

It was like the crashing of waves from two sides against a rock, but Holmes stood as silent and unmoved as the rock itself. And the firmness of the rock made an impression.

"You wouldn't mind if I locked the girls in their bedrooms?" Miss Ingrahm continued after a moment's silence.

"In that case, they didn't need to know anything about what was going on," her friend added.

"You were supposed to stay in the corridor, sir?"

"We sometimes let the woodcutter and the gas fitter in there."

"You can't risk your life either."

"Who can ask to be robbed and murdered?"

"It is my duty, for Molly's sake, to get to the bottom of this."

"You don't have the right, Ciss, to let the child entrusted to you be kidnapped when you can prevent it."

"So, Mr Holmes, you and the doctor will be joining us after dark?"

With this question from Miss Ingrahm, the matter was settled, and in a short time, my friend and I were able to leave the sanctuary of female virtue and innocence, the Institute at Glower street, with the intention of returning there in the evening.

If, to use Miss Sladd's poetic imagery, the "stars of heaven" had looked in at the window of the lower corridor of the Ingrahm Institute - which, however, they did not, for the autumn evening was overcast and misty - their thousands of beaming eyes would have seen a sight that might have made them hide modestly behind the clouds: two men, Holmes and I, seated in comfortable armchairs in the said corridor, while the ladies Ingrahm and Sladd, closely pressed together in the former's neighbouring reception room, awaited the progress of events under extreme nervous tension. Everything in the house was plunged into silence; all the lights had been switched off as usual at half past nine, and teachers and pupils were locked up in their respective bedrooms like prisoners in their cells. Some very faint sounds, however, but still quite audible to my keen ear, led me to suspect that the female inhabitants of the house were not in the deep sleep of blissful ignorance, but that a presentiment of some strange and important event was keeping them awake. It was impossible for any connoisseur of female nature - and as a married man of four years standing, I had some experience - to suppose that little Alice could have resisted the temptation to tell them what she knew about the disguised woman - and then some. The unusual measure of locking the bedrooms and the nervous excitement of the ladies Ingrahm and Sladd also set in motion a host of youthful fantasies.

How many hours of wakefulness and excitement I had spent by my friend's side! What I actually did with it I have always found difficult to understand. My role has almost always been limited to that of a passive spectator, but I suppose my presence had a stimulating effect on my friend's mental faculties, much as the cheering of spectators encourages participants in a running or pole-vaulting competition to exert themselves to the utmost. This time, however, my influence was probably slight, for my weak nature could not resist the triple temptation of nocturnal stillness, nocturnal sleepiness, and a comfortable recliner. I fell asleep.

I didn't know how long I had been asleep, but I was woken up by a rather thin and angular hand touching my arm. "It's time!" a barely audible voice whispered in my ear. I realised, however, that the voice and hand belonged to Miss Ingrahm.

She had not been able to remain in the parlour, nor had her faithful friend, when their keen hearing picked up the faint rattle of a key being inserted into the lock of the front door from outside. I too heard the same rattle. Miss Ingrahm was right: the moment had come.

Gently, almost inaudibly, the key was turned in the lock, and similarly the door was opened. Footsteps, light as the gentle whisper of a wind fan across a lawn, approached. We listened with bated breath. Was it one person approaching, or several? It couldn't possibly be more than one, obviously the woman in disguise. We had all risen at the first sound of the door-lock being moved; Holmes took the place nearest the direction from which the mysterious person was to come, I took a step back towards the wall; behind me stood Miss Ingrahm, Miss Sladd behind my friend. The intruding criminal - for that is what the disguised woman must be regarded as - could not fail to fall into our power.

Carefully examining the terrain, she advanced the few metres that separated us from the front door; she drew nearer and nearer, I heard her breathing - then a bright light blazed across the corridor - the glow of Holmes' electric torch. A triple scream of shrill female voices echoed through the corridor; at the same moment everything was plunged into black darkness, some object fell rattling to the floor, I heard Holmes' angry voice: "Are you mad, man! Let go, I say! Run, Watson, catch her!" I heard fleeing footsteps, and saw against the darkness of the doorway an even darker shadow, and realised that our prey was escaping us. Without hesitation I rushed towards the exit, while behind me I heard the noise of doors being flung open, the trampling of a number of feet, and the unruly clamour of voices.

I came out into the garden; the sound of the fugitive's footsteps guided me; she headed for the side facing the park. Again I heard the sound of her short, sharp breaths and realised that I was gaining ground. I reached out my hand and grabbed the air at random, but was lucky enough to catch hold of something warm and soft - a woman's arm. It twisted in violent movements, but I held on. A voice, soft and beautiful in the midst of its agitation, called out to me half-aloud: "Oh, let me go! I have done nothing wrong!"

Was I unwillingly mesmerised by the beautiful, pleading voice, or did it distract my attention? I don't know, only that with a sudden jerk the woman's arm was torn from my grasp, and the next moment she had disappeared behind a bush. I followed as fast and as well as I could, but bewildered at my recent inattention, I took the wrong road and stumbled against a chestnut tree. But at the same moment a voice next to me called out, "There she is!" and a bright, pale blue light illuminated part of the outer edge of the garden. In this light, I saw a figure hurry towards the fence, pause for a second, and cast a searching glance behind her, whereupon she seized hold of a couple of the upright ribs of the fence, and with a movement as smooth as it was elegant, swung herself over the fence and disappeared into the park.

As she turned around, I caught a glimpse of the face and figure of the 'woman in disguise.' Fleeting as this glimpse was, it left a clear image in my mind. Such is the power of beauty, and beauty of the highest order characterised both her features and her figure; both possessed the highest, almost classical perfection. But especially the look in her large, light brown eyes burned into my mind, a look at once fearful and defiant and so deeply sad, almost tearingly despairing.

Truly moved by a kind of compassion, I stood by the tree rubbing my forehead, where a large bump testified to my over-eager acquaintance with the chestnut when I was awakened to the reality by the voice close to me, which had just spoken.

"That's it! That's the end of the adventure! We might as well go inside now, sir!"

I looked around. The speaker was little Alice, standing there, letting my friend Holmes' electric lamp create various light effects among the bushes and trees of the garden.

"You here, little one?" I asked, surprised. "How did you get here?"

"On my legs, of course!" she replied cheekily.

"But how did you get out of your room?"

Alice looked me sharply in the face. "Do you promise not to tell if I tell?"

I felt interested in the little rascal. "I promise."

"I believe you because you are a man. Men can be trusted, but not women. Women can't keep their mouths shut, and they're so terribly false; they're just like cats."

I did wonder where Miss Ingrahm's favourite pupil got the material for this idea of the characteristics of the sexes, but I said aloud: "You were supposed to tell me."

"Well, sir, this is how it happened. Miss Ingrahm thought she could fool us, of course, and pretended that everything was going on as usual, let us say our evening prayers and put out the lights and lock ourselves in. But she was deceiving herself; we are not idiots, and I had been allowed to peek behind the scenes and did not keep quiet about what I knew. We had a feeling that something very exciting was going to happen tonight, especially when we heard you and that other policeman's voices whispering in the corridor with Miss Ciss and the

Echo, as we call Miss Sladd. They thought we were going to go to sleep! No way in hell! Sitting locked up, when it's so easy to pick the bad locks with a penknife! Never came into question. When they started shouting in the corridor, we couldn't hold it any longer and rushed out, and I was just in time to see Miss Sladd throw her arms round your friend the policeman and shout, 'Oh God, I'm dying! Save me!' Your friend couldn't move a hand but dropped the lamp, you ran out of the door after the fugitive, and I followed you, but accidentally stepped on something. Immediately, it struck me: 'That's the lamp'; and it was, and I picked it up. There you have the whole story. But now let's go inside! There's probably a lot of fun going on there that we shouldn't miss."

I did not know what to admire most in little Alice: her presence of mind, her developed perception of things and people, or the results of the Ingrahm Institute's famous art of education. I left the question unanswered and followed the girl into the house.

Miss Ingrahm was restoring order and calm to the agitated crowd of young girls, teachers and pupils gathered in the corridor and trying to get them out of there and into the bedrooms. Miss Sladd sat in an armchair with her head bowed in her hands like a Niobe picture of crushing grief, while my friend Holmes paced back and forth with his hands in his pockets, whispering indifferently.

"There you are, Watson," he said when he recognised my arrival. "The bird has flown? I couldn't believe it. Let's go home and go to bed. The show is over. Perhaps it was intended as a tragedy but ended as a farce. Miss Sladd has played the heroine brilliantly, I assure you. I give her my compliments."

"Alas, Mr Holmes, how can you have the heart to say so?" complained the said lady from the armchair.

"You've been acting like a fool, like an idiot, Val. I am ashamed of myself because of you. You have spoilt everything; you have caused a scandal, and that in my house, in the Ingrahm Institute!"

It was her friend's voice that so comforted the unhappy Miss Sladd. Doubly devastated, she sobbed:

"What have I done? I was just scared."

"You have, perhaps forever, prevented the solution of a most interesting and intricate mystery," replied Holmes.

"You have hugged the policeman there; you have; I saw it."

Who else but little Alice Drebber uttered these amiable and respectful words, which, by the way, were rather too rash to come from such a quick-witted and perceptive person, for they led to her being driven out of the corridor and thus losing the opportunity to witness the further development of things.

This did not last long, by the way. My friend Mr Holmes turned to Miss Ingrahm and said: "I consider my work in this affair to be finished. I have no wish to expose myself to further incidents like the one that has just occurred. One piece of advice, however, Miss: telegraph tomorrow morning to Count Valricco - he is in Brighton, I am assured at his embassy - that he will immediately fetch his ward Molly from here and take her to a safer place, if he cares for her at all. Do not delay, Miss, unless you wish to see your honourable institution exposed to a greater calamity and scandal than that which has threatened it tonight."

My friend left, and I followed.

As we later learnt, Miss Ingrahm followed my friend's advice to the letter. The very next day, Count Valricco arrived from Brighton and took little Molly Nessle away from the Institute, where, we never learnt.

*

THE affair at the Ingrahm Institute had almost been forgotten when, on an August day the following year, Holmes received the following telegram:

Please come immediately without delay to Fasham near Brighton for a consultation of the highest importance. Count Valricco."

Holmes went to my home, but did not find me there. My wife and I had gone on a visit to acquaintances and would be away till the next day. He left me a few lines asking me to follow him as soon as possible; he felt that his journey could not be delayed. What I am telling you here about the first stage of the case is therefore based on my friend's information.

Fasham is a small fishing village on the coast of the English Channel, about five kilometres from Brighton. The Albanian ambassador to the English court, Count Valricco, had a delightful villa just on the edge of the village. The Count was a tall, somewhat lean gentleman of distinctly aristocratic appearance and diplomatically genteel manners, about 55 years old and unmarried. The parties he gave in London during the season were said to be splendid, but in the country, he lived a rather retired life without a large staff.

Holmes arrived at Fasham shortly after lunch and was immediately received by the Count, who was obviously in a very agitated state.

"Mr Holmes, you are most welcome, and I am grateful that you responded so quickly to my summons. I expect everything from your recognised acumen."

"What is the matter?" Holmes asked.

"I have lost a paper of the utmost importance, a letter from one of Europe's leading statesmen."

"When?"

"Early this morning. I get up early and work; early mornings are golden, Mr Holmes. So, too, today. I was in the act of answering the said letter, and had it before me on the desk by the window. The latter I had open as usual to enjoy the fresh sea air. Whilst working, I happened to glance down into the garden and discovered that my terrier puppy 'Bird' was rampaging through my groups of cactus dahlias. These are currently my passions, and I was very worried that they would be destroyed before I could send someone to chase the dog away. So I ran down the stairs and out into the garden myself, chased Bird away and returned to my study.

Imagine my dismay and concern when I found all the other papers on the desk still there, but the important letter was gone."

"Do you suspect that someone might have entered the room in your absence and stolen the paper?" Holmes asked.

"Impossible. The lock on the door is designed to lock itself when you close the door from the outside, and I well remember doing that and even hearing the click that confirms the lock is closing."

"But a false key?" Holmes suggested.

"Absolutely out of the question. You see, Mr Holmes, a diplomat like me, especially in the present situation, must take every possible precaution to protect his papers. I am in the habit of changing the lock of my study from time to time, but never at fixed times. The new locks always have a completely different mechanism, and it is quite complicated. They are ordered from a Milan-based locksmith, sent in a registered parcel, and no one but myself screws them into place. One such new lock arrived just last night. A theft of the letter is unthinkable."

Holmes noted to himself that the Count was either an extraordinarily cautious diplomat or engaged in unusually secretive affairs, but said aloud:

"And the roof, walls and floors...?"

"I have examined everything very carefully myself; not a trace of anything unusual."

Holmes could not help saying, "Your Excellency, you hardly seem to need my help; you are your own detective."

"I am an experienced diplomat, sir; as such, one learns various things, above all to observe - and suspect."

"Do you have any theory on the matter?" Holmes asked.

"I have; a theory which seems to me the only possible one. When I hastily opened or closed the door, the letter may have been blown out of the window by the draught and fallen into the garden."

"You've been looking for that."

"Of course. For over an hour. I've searched every inch - the garden is quite small. But without results, without a single clue."

"Who helped you with the search?"

"Helped? Do you consider me such an idiot, sir, that I would enlist the help of any of the servants to look for such a letter? Apart from the fact that they could find and hide it, their trampling and rummaging would make an examination by an expert like you impossible. I have taken the utmost care to make my traces as few but as clear as possible, and have had the garden closed up so that everything would be untouched until you arrived."

"Permit me to express my admiration for wisdom and thoughtfulness which are exceedingly rare in my field of experience. If the world were full of your ilk, the detective's profession would soon become a breadless occupation," said Holmes. "And how do the servants take what has happened?"

"You surprise me, Mr Holmes. I thought, after what I've said and you've said, you wouldn't think me narrow-minded enough to let the staff have even an inkling of my loss. I have justified the closure of the garden with Bird's destruction of my dahlias."

"One more question, Your Excellency. It may seem indiscreet, but it is necessary if my forthcoming investigation is not to be left in the dark. You know the saying: 'Who did it? Well, the person who benefited from it. I must ask you: what was in the letter?"

"I understand you and will tell you all I can. It contained state secrets of the highest importance, proposals which touched not only the deepest interests of my own country and England, but those of a few other great powers. If the letter should fall into certain hands or be published in the press, not only would my own position be completely undermined, but there would be a danger of a great, perhaps European, war. I dare not go further in my revelations, not even to you."

Holmes stood up.

"I think I have the information I need, at least for the moment, and with your Honour's permission, I will begin my work. Just one more question: what does the letter look like?"

"White, fairly thin postal paper, largest format, tightly compressed style on all four sides, no monogram or other mark. Both my name and the sender's name were printed in full."

Holmes began his work. After spending half an hour in a careful examination of the little garden, he turned to the Count with the following question:

"Does Your Excellency usually give his cast-off shoes to the valet or the gardener?"

The Count held out his well-shod foot: "Do you think any of them could wear shoes like these? Their feet must be at least an inch bigger than mine."

"In that case, no one except yourself and the dog has been in the garden today. Nor has a letter been able to blow outside its area by the wind; the tall trees around make it impossible. May I beg your pardon for a piece of bread or a piece of meat?"

"Of course, I'd love to, but I don't understand..."

"If your theory that the letter was blown out of the window by the draught is correct - and so far I believe it is - then the thief has been found. There can be only one person on whom suspicion falls: Bird, the dog."

"Bird? Ah, you are right. Bird is so playful and has a great fondness for fetching things, especially paper, which he plays with and tears to pieces. Mr Holmes, you cannot imagine the relief your words bring to my troubled mind."

"Your Excellency! It is probable that Bird brought the letter; it is possible that he bit it to pieces while playing, but it is equally possible that someone took the letter from him and hid it, for what purpose we do not know. The dog tracks show that after you chased Bird away from the dahlias, he hid behind the large group of hydrangeas, then came to the vicinity of the building and from there went out through the west gate - you used the east one. It is Bird's behaviour after he left the garden that must now be investigated."

"I will accompany you myself and familiarise you with Bird," said the Count.

Bird's tracks from the garden were not easy to follow; they went in several nooks and crannies and were often obliterated by the servants' footprints. They seemed, however, to lead to a small backyard where the servants kept some rubbish. The two gentlemen directed their steps there.

Suddenly, the Count gave an exclamation. Turning around, Sherlock Holmes, who had been searching elsewhere, saw the diplomat waving a small piece of paper between his fingers. It was quite insignificant, about five or six centimetres on each side, crumpled and dirty.

"It's a corner of the letter," the Count whispered angrily to the detective. "Here are some letters, only a few, but I recognise them. You are an astute man, Mr Holmes. You were right: the dog has obviously got hold of the letter."

"Let's see what else we can find," Holmes replied briefly.

He had scarcely uttered the words when he took a few steps to one side, stooped down and picked up a piece of paper, exactly like the one just found, evidently the same corner but from the other sheet. The search now continued with redoubled zeal, every spot of the backyard and the objects therein being carefully examined, but without further result. Equally fruitless was the search of the courtyard, the short avenue, the viewing kiosk and the doghouse. Fortunately, the grounds of the villa were not very extensive, and the Count was able to certify that the dog had been neither outside its limits nor inside the house; for as soon as the master discovered his loss, he had Bird tied to the dog-house, so that he might not enter the garden and destroy any traces there.

Holmes' face became very serious.

"Does Bird often hang out in the backyard?" he asked.

"It's his favourite outdoor place."

"Well, Your Excellency, I fear that the situation is as bad as possible. I think we can establish the sequence of events something like this: the dog saw the letter flying in the air and falling to the ground; he grabbed one of its corners with his teeth and ran to the backyard to hide his prey or play with it. There he has met one of the servants - no one else visits that place - this someone has snatched the letter from the dog - the broken edge suggests such a snatching - probably at first with no other intention than to save it from the dog's advance, but has then read it and realised its value. The person must, therefore, have had a certain degree of education and acumen to recognise the value of the document. To whom among your servants do you attribute these qualities? Your chamberlain?"

"Berti has a clever head, but he can't read handwriting, let alone print. I think I am best served by a servant who lacks these skills."

"And your other servants?"

"The butler hardly condescends to visit the backyard, nor does the housekeeper. I hardly know the other servants by name only; I have only a few servants out here: the serving maid, the cook, the two maids."

"And nothing remarkable has happened among the staff today?"

"Nothing, as far as I know. I take little notice of such things. Mr Davis, the butler, manages the lower servants at his pleasure and to my satisfaction."

"Would you be so kind as to allow me to speak to Mr Davis in your office and in your presence?"

Five minutes later, the maître d', a greasy-looking, authoritatively good-natured fellow, stood in the cabinet. Holmes addressed him.

"Mr Davis! The Count has authorised me to ask you some questions. I represent a company which is planning to open a first-class hotel in London - His Excellency has shown an interest in the project - and we need servants who are accustomed to the manners and services of finer houses. The Count has authorised me to ask you if there are any among the staff here whom you consider suitable and willing to take employment with us."

Mr Davis raised his eyebrows thoughtfully. "The cook, sir, I'm sure won't leave her place, and the server, sir, well, not that I want to say anything against him, but he has a manner, sir, that I'm sure you wouldn't like, I'd almost say a little silly, and he likes to stick his nose in everything. Lucy, the other maid, is a pretty girl, but a little stupid, sir, and lacks the elegance that must be demanded of a first-class servant; besides, she won't move if the footman stays; there's a little courtship between them, while it lasts, for the footman changes the objects of his courtship as others change waistcoats, he's a real Don Juan. On the other hand, I might have recommended Deborah, if she were still here, our first maid, sir, a very good girl, but, as I say, she is not here, so we can't count on her."

"Where has she moved to?" Holmes asked.

"I don't know, sir. I suppose she hasn't got a seat yet. She only left this morning."

"Oh, she left? For what reason? You see, Mr Davis, I would very much like to employ a woman of your recommendation, but I need to know more about her character."

"She left the service because she felt insulted. After breakfast, she dropped a silver tray on the floor, leaving a large dent; when I reprimanded her for the mistake, she replied nastily, whereupon I gave her another reprimand. This upset her, and she hurled insults at me and asked to be dismissed from her post, which, in the circumstances, I did not hesitate to give her. She was so angry that she even refused my offer of a lift to Brighton."

"So she had a very hot temper, this Debora?"

"I cannot say that, sir. Until today, she has always been willing, docile and content. I don't understand what got into her."

"Thank you, Mr Davis, for the information, even if it did not produce any results. You realise that Debora is not suited to the position I have in mind. Too hot-tempered, sir, too hot-tempered."

When the maître d' left, Holmes said:

"I think we are one step closer to the missing letter, Your Excellency. I would be surprised if Debora's sudden change of mood and cancellation of a good post were not connected with your loss. It is Deborah's trail that we must follow, and it will not be easy because we are dealing with a clever head who has also been given a three or four-hour head start. A woman who realises the importance of a diplomatic letter, who doesn't just run away but comes up with a plausible explanation for her departure, and who, by refusing a lift, forces us to waste time tracking her down, is no ordinary maid. The more I look into it, the more serious it seems. But I have no time to lose. See you later, Count!"

Holmes went to the village, where he engaged in seemingly meaningless conversations with the inhabitants.

Eventually, he managed to find out how and where Deborah had travelled: a farmer had taken her to the railway station in Lewes, from where he had just returned. Twenty minutes later, Sherlock Holmes was on his way to that town.

However, the chances of finding the Fasham housekeeper were very slim, especially as this part of England is crossed by an extensive railway network. Holmes only had a photograph as a clue, which Deborah had sent to Mr Davis when she applied for the Count's job. Nor could he find any information about the whereabouts of a woman of her appearance in Lewes. Dissatisfied, Holmes decided to return to Fasham, but first went to the telegraph station to send a telegram.

While writing down the message, he happened to glance at the pad laid out for correspondents to use when writing telegrams. It was new for the day and bore scarcely a trace of use, only a few lines having left an imprint. In these lines, my friend fixated on a word which, in a mirrored script, of course, appeared to be the name, Deborah. Was it a mistake or was fate giving him a clue? He didn't know which, because he couldn't make out the mirrored and rather indistinct writing on the substrate. He handed in his telegram and left, but returned a few minutes later with a small hand mirror. Using it, he was now able to read in right-angled script: "Miss Flory White! Circus Caruzzi. Dover. Meet me tonight at 9 train at Ashford. Victory. Debora."

Even Holmes's usually unperturbed state of mind was disturbed by this unexpected turn of events. There could hardly be any doubt that the Deborah he sought was the one who had sent the telegram message. He wrote a telegram summoning me to Ashford as soon as possible and left the station.

I did not return from my journey until the next morning, but immediately got on the train to Ashford, where I went to see my friend at the hotel he had indicated. He received me very kindly.

"It is a pity, Watson, that I did not have you here last night, a great pity indeed, for you could have been of invaluable assistance." After recounting the events at Fasham as I have described them above, he continued:

"I bought a ticket for Ashford and got there a few minutes before the arrival of the train from Dover, so I had time to orientate myself at the station. The sun had just set, but a clear evening glow replaced its light, and it was still full daylight. Some people were waiting on the platform for the train to arrive, and I searched the crowd for someone who looked like Deborah's photograph. Sure enough, there she was the young woman in the tight-fitting dark blue, simple suit and with the not beautiful but rather sympathetic face. In her hand she held a small bag with steel fittings; perhaps the fateful letter was there, the one on which the peace of Europe might depend. I felt an overwhelming desire to snatch the bag and examine its contents. Still, of course, I had to restrain myself - otherwise, my fate would have been the less desirable one of being arrested and put in Ashford prison as a thief. At the same moment the train roared into the station, I was crowding nearer and nearer to her whom I supposed to be my Deborah, when a terrible jolt from behind threw me forward on the wooden pavement. I had been so busy watching the girl that I had neither noticed the arrival of the baggage carriage with the luggage nor listened to the warning shouts of the station attendants. The shock was strong, and it was a few minutes before I could overcome the pain and look around to see something. The arriving passengers had already left the train and started streaming out of the station. Naturally, I threw myself into the crowd, looked people in the face in the most foolish way, handed out and received pushes galore, and searched waiting rooms and restaurants, but all in vain. Finally, when I had already given up hope, I happened to glance through the window into the ladies' waiting room, and there on the sofa sat my Debora next to a young, radiantly beautiful woman, no doubt Miss Flory White. On this day my luck was threefold; there could be no doubt that I was on the right track and close to my goal: the letter. But how was I to get it? Using force was unthinkable. Besides, the ladies' waiting room was a forbidden place for me. And which of the women had the letter? They had had at least ten or fifteen minutes to meet without me being able to observe them, and what could have happened in that time? I had to settle for the role of observer from a distance.

The two women sat in their seats for over an hour. Suddenly they got up and went to the ticket office; I hurried after them and bought a ticket for Canterbury, which I had no intention of using, but in this way, I managed to hear Deborah ask for a ticket for Maidstone, while the beauty, whom I supposed to be Flory, bought a ticket for Dover. A few minutes later I saw them going their separate ways.

Now you see, Watson, why I regretted that you were not here last night. I needed to investigate the whereabouts of both women, but I couldn't split up and go in two directions. If you had been here, you could have followed one while I followed the other.

I had to choose, and I did. I chose Miss Flory. You wonder why? But by all common sense, it had to be. Flory must have the letter. Deborah had evidently taken employment in the Count's house with a definite intention, and Flory was aware of that intention; the word 'victory' in the telegram proves it. If Deborah had stolen the letter for her own account and use, she would not have risked staying for hours in a place as near Brighton as Ashford; she would have hurried away with her booty as far and as fast as possible. There is only one explanation for her coming here and meeting Flory: she wanted to deliver the letter to the latter. Flory is the protagonist. Deborah is the tool. What the purpose of the plot might be is still unclear, but I have shed light into darker darkness. Don't think, however, Watson, that I am going to let Debora out of my sight. She evidently intends to spend the night at Maidstone, and she will find one of my aides at her heels in the morning. I have telegraphed and given him a detailed description of her. But you and I, Doctor, are going to Dover to see a performance tonight at the Circus Caruzzi; perhaps you will see the Ambassador, Count Valricco, there. I have already telegraphed for him this morning."

Such was the story of my friend Holmes. After a light meal, we travelled to Dover.

The Caruzzi Circus had a fairly full theatre. The second row, where my friend Mr Holmes and I were seated, was completely full, but the front row had considerable gaps. The performance was not bad for a country troupe, and the applause was lively. Of course, my friend and I watched the performance with little interest as we were anxiously awaiting Miss Flory's appearance.

Finally, her first act arrived: a display of dressage by two little lion cubs, the cutest creatures imaginable, barely much bigger than kittens.

Miss Flory was dressed in a thin, light-green costume which clung closely to her lithe, ideal form. Illuminated by the artificial light of the stage, she was ravishingly beautiful, and her beauty was not of that banal, challenging kind which often characterises circus ladies but carried it over as it were a veil of decency, gentleness and melancholy.

At first sight, I involuntarily flinched: I had seen this face before, and especially these eyes, so light brown, gentle and sad. But where? I did not notice Miss Flory and her tricks after that, I just wondered: "Where have I seen her before?"

The act ended with a theatrical effect: suddenly, the whole stage was darkened, but over Flory, a spotlight cast its dazzling light. With her arms hanging at her sides, she stood motionless like a statue of beauty, while the two lion cubs lay equally motionless at her feet.

Thunderous applause and enthusiastic cheers rewarded the beautiful scene, but in the midst of the noise, I heard my friend's voice whispering in my ear: "I was right! She has the letter."

I looked at him questioningly. What could give him this security? He understood my silent question and said: "Watson! Did you see the sharply squared but almost imperceptible ridge in the silk covering her breast? You didn't notice it, but I saw it through my binoculars, because I was looking for it - women have a weakness for hiding their valuables in that very spot. And when the spotlight fell on it, I saw how the silk right there turned out a shade lighter than usual. She has the letter!"

I was only half attentive to my friend's words, for I had also made a surprising observation. The sudden burst of light from the spotlight recalled to my mind the curious scene in the garden of the Ingrahm Institute, when little Alice Drebber, with Holmes's torch, illuminated the flight of the "disguised woman" over the fence, and all at once it was clear to me where I had seen Miss Flory's face: she and the "disguised woman" were the same person. No two people in the world could possess the same unusual beauty, much less eyes with such an expression.

Of the following acts, equestrianism and acrobatics, I understood nothing, for a series of questions crowded my mind. What could Miss Flory be doing at the Ingrahm Institute? Could the tutor there, Debora Westrow, be the same person as the housemaid Debora in Fasham? As I remembered, Count Valricco had been mentioned as little Molly Nessle's patron; in a curious way the events seemed to connect all the persons mentioned, Deborah, Flory, and the Count, with both the Ingrahm Institute and Fasham, with the events of about a year ago and the events of now; but what was the connection?

Again my thoughts were disturbed by the whisper of my friend Holmes. This time, he pointed down the front row, on whose front bench sat, quite alone by himself, a tall, lean gentleman with a genteel appearance. "There is Count Valricco," Holmes announced. "He has just come in."

At the same moment, behind the circus stage, there was a low rumbling and a great roar; a huge iron cage was brought into the centre of the arena; its occupants, three stately lions, expressed by their thunderous noises their dissatisfaction with the journey or with the work they knew to be in store for them. Immediately afterwards Miss Flory entered, made a short bow to the audience, and then entered the lions' cage.

With a feeling of horror, I turned my eyes away from the spectacle in the arena. This beautiful, gentle creature among these ravenous beasts! Would they not crush her with their claws, grind her perfect limbs to dust between their terrible teeth?

But none of this happened. The beasts were subdued by her glances; they obeyed her slightest beckonings; they shrank away trembling and frightened when she raised her supple riding stick; they willingly performed their tricks, and they stroked themselves caressingly at her feet. And she walked among the wild beasts so calmly, smiled so sweetly, moved as gracefully as if she had danced across the parquet of a ballroom.

But suddenly I saw her pale and, with an involuntary movement, bring her hand to her heart. Even her lips had whitened, and her figure trembled convulsively. She stood in the centre of the group of lions, facing the spectators, so that I could observe every change in her features. What was going on? Did she feel she was losing her power over the beasts? Did she sense a terrible accident? My heart began to beat wildly.

Once again, I heard Holmes whisper: "She recognises him! She has seen the Count!" I saw her eyes fixed on him. That is why she has faded. Things are getting more and more interesting.

Holmes was undoubtedly right, he had a remarkable acumen. But what a hardened heart, what a detective's view of the matter! What did he care for the anxiety and pain of this beautiful creature? He was indifferent to everything except his investigations.

This was the last act of the show, and Holmes rose hastily: "I'm going down to catch the Count. Follow me, Watson, to the first-row exit, when the crowd has had time to pour out."

He left, and I could watch Flory. She had regained her composure and received the applause of the spectators with a smile before leaving the lion cage.

On leaving the front row, I found my friend in conversation with an aristocratic gentleman, who was introduced to me as Count Valricco. At the conclusion of a conversation between the two men, Holmes uttered:

"As you wish then, Mr. Count. It makes no difference whether we settle it tonight or tomorrow."

We went up to the circus arena itself without hindrance; Holmes had prepared our entrance. The gas lamps were being extinguished; only a few were still burning, leaving the vast room in semi-darkness. One performer after another hurried away in haste; from the neighbouring stables came the stamping of horses, the roaring of wild beasts, and the shouts of the staff. In the arena, the large lion cage remained, and everything else was left as it was during the performance. We lingered a while in impatient expectation, so said the Count:

"As long as she doesn't escape us!"

"Impossible," replied my friend. "I have ascertained from the porter that she is still in her dressing-room, and that there is no other exit from it than across the arena. She was the last to appear, and will therefore, probably be the last to leave. And it may be as well for our settlement."

It was some fifteen minutes before she arrived, dressed in a simple black suit, but no less charming than in her stage costume. She was halfway across the arena when Holmes stood in her way.

"Excuse me, Miss White! But I must ask for a word with you."

She looked at him in surprise.

"About what? Here? And now?"

"Yes, Miss, here and now. My name is Sherlock Holmes; perhaps you know it?"

"The great detective?"

"Yes, Miss. And I request that you hand over a letter that has fallen into your hands, a letter to Count Valricco."

At that moment, the Count emerged from the shadows where he had hitherto been hidden.

"Yes, give me the letter, the letter you stole, you impostor, you thief, you..."

The bitterness choked the words from his throat; his face was white with excitement. Even Miss Flory turned pale.

"Ah, you're here! Well, I should have guessed it. You call me a thief; you do! What shall I call you then?"

She stepped almost menacingly close to the Count. Sherlock Holmes stepped between them.

"Miss, for your own good, I urge you to hand over the letter in question to Mr Count. You have it in your possession."

"And if I refuse?"

"Then I must use force. I will arrest you."

"You would use force? Mr Holmes, don't you realise that a shout from me would bring a dozen circus workers to my defence? Arrest me? Well, then the letter would have to be handed over to the police, and you wouldn't want that, would you, Count Valricco? I don't understand politics, but I've been told by someone with insight that this is the last thing you would want."

The Count made a gesture of impotent resentment, but Holmes interjected: "The matter has been placed in my hands, Miss. My honour as a detective demands

that I complete the task. I shall have the letter, for good
or ill, wherever you may have hidden it."

Flory smiled.

"You are clever and strong, Mr Holmes, but where
the letter is kept you dare not go. Let us see it! I will
show you the hiding place myself."

Before anyone could stop her, she opened the lion's
cage and entered, after which she went into the lions'
actual room.

In the centre of it was an iron pillar, shaped at the
top like a small box, in which Flory kept various small
things, a revolver, thorny necklaces, a motley veil, and
so on, which she used in her scenes with the lions. She
now opened this box and took out a piece of paper.

"Here is the letter, Mr Holmes; here is your
document, Count!" she said triumphantly as she held
up the paper.

Involuntarily, the defendants had approached the
bars of the cage to see the precious paper, but even more
involuntarily, they took a couple of great, hasty leaps
backwards. Two of the lions had rushed up to the bars
with terrible roars and tried to push their huge paws
through.

"Back off, Leo, calm down, Laila!" Flory urged them
as she calmly put the letter back in the drawer, which
she closed with a mechanism. After calming the animals,
she came out to us.

"There is no one but myself and Mrs. Dravitsky who
dares to go into Leo and Laila, and she is at present in
South America, I know not where. Do you still think,

Mr Holmes, that you can get your hands on the letter without my consent?"

I saw in my friend's face the unusual expression of wantonness and humiliation; but the count could no longer restrain his anger.

"You devil, do you want to destroy me?"

"And if I did, who could blame me?" Flory replied proudly. "And I would," she added passionately, "if you had no hold on me. Therefore, I will compromise: give me back my child, and I will give you your letter."

"A compromise? A child?" Holmes said in surprise. "What do you mean, Miss?"

"That one knows what I mean." Flory nodded his head towards the Count. The Count was pacing back and forth with rapid steps in a strong internal struggle. Suddenly he stopped and turned to Flory:

"You have played a daring game, Florence, but it looks as if you have won - for the moment at least." He turned to Holmes. "Mr Holmes! I leave the matter in your hands; just get me the letter back. I'll agree to any compromise you like. Just get me the letter and get it tonight! I'm staying at the Pas de Calais Hotel."

With these words, the Count hurriedly left. Sherlock Holmes looked after him, completely surprised.

"Miss White!" He said after a pause. "It seems that there are deeper waters to be fathomed here than I realised. You have heard the words of the Count. On what terms will you release the paper?"

"Mr Holmes! You have witnessed for yourself that I have the right and power to dictate whatever terms I wish. But this is not enough for me. I will not have an undeserved shadow cast over me; you shall know why I have acted as I have done, and that my seizure of the letter was only a justifiable self-defence. You shall hear my story before we decide on the matter. But this is not the place for it. Come with me to my lodgings at the Strand Hotel opposite; there, you shall know all."

Ten minutes later, my friend and I were sitting in Miss Flory's interview room, and she started telling her story.

"I was born in England. My father was called Leoni and owned a famous circus in his day; my mother was English. From an early age I performed in the theatre, but I also received a good education for my profession - it was my mother's will. At the age of 16, I became an orphan and was left without shelter and money in the world. Then, I joined the Caruzzi Circus, where I was trained as a rider. By chance, I discovered my talent as a tamer of wild animals; from the age of 18, it became my job.

During our stay in Milan, I became acquainted with Alberto Valricco, not the Count's diplomat, but his nephew, the head of the family and owner of their vast estate. He saw me and was seized with a fierce love; I loved him too, and within six months, I was his wife, the wife of the highborn nobleman.

Our marriage was happy; those were the brightest summer days of my life. My Alberto did not love society and the splendours of the great world; he was an introvert by nature and a lover of study. With a few servants, we lived in a small villa, we lived in a small villa a few miles from Nice, delightfully situated in relative seclusion from other people's neighbourhood; 'Le nid' was its apt name. Here, our child was born; Molly was called after my mother.

Our happiness was rich and deep but short. My husband's sudden illness and death was the first blow that hit me. Molly was then only three months old.

Alberto's illness was typhoid; I nursed him to his last breath, but immediately afterwards, I fell ill with the same terrible disease. For weeks, I lay unconscious, but my inherent vitality prevailed, and one day, I was strong enough to leave my bed.

Nature was in its richest splendour; the oranges shimmered in gold between the dark leaves, and the scent of roses hit me through the open window. I felt as if I had been reborn! Despite my sadness, life was still good to live.

But my baby! My Molly! Where was she? Why wasn't she brought to me? My Alberto was gone, but I still had my Molly.

The blow came suddenly, numbingly. For three weeks, my child had been resting in the cemetery in the village up in the mountains. The same disease that had slain her father and brought her mother to the brink of the grave had also cut the thread of her life.

Was it because the blow came so numbingly upon the already weak, that it was not crushing? My soul was as if in hibernation, but my body recovered surprisingly quickly, both in health and strength.

Then, one day, a man dressed in black and accompanied by two policemen turned up. He introduced himself as a notary and came on behalf of Count Valricco, my late husband's uncle. This uncle was now, after my husband's death, the head of the dynasty and had succeeded to the estate by virtue of a provision which stipulated that if, at the time of death, the holder had no heirs, the property would pass undivided to the nearest blood relative. Out of respect for his nephew's memory, the Count, despite his disapproval of his nephew's remarriage, nevertheless wished to grant the widow possession of the villa and an annual allowance of 3 000 francs.

Such was the notary's presentation. In my weakened state of mind, I wished only for tranquillity, and accepted the count's offer with gratitude. I needed so little; a single maid was enough for me.

Three months passed in peace; eventually, my mental health and vigour were also restored. I would really need it!

One day I was called to Marina's sickbed. She was an old woman from the Genoa area who had served the Valricco family for years, most recently at 'Le nid,' my villa, but had moved on when the household broke up and was now living in a cottage a few kilometres from the villa. I had never liked her and had perhaps, unwisely, shown it too clearly. Her appearance was repulsive to me.

When I arrived, she was dying, and under the impression of the nearness of death, she made a horrifying confession: my child, my Molly, was not dead but alive. During my illness, Valricco, the ambassador, had arrived at the villa on the pretext of looking after his deceased nephew's fortune. In a short time, he had convinced Marina of his plans; she agreed, attracted by the promise of a large reward and by hatred for me. The Count made her little Molly's guardian and one day; it was announced that the child had also fallen ill with typhus, and a few days later she had died. A coffin was procured, and the Count declared that the child, as a descendant of Valricco, should be buried in the family vault on the main estate; he travelled, taking the little coffin with him.

But a few stations away, in the dark of night, Marina appeared with Molly, whom she handed over to the Count, received her reward and returned home before daybreak.

I heard the old woman's confession without believing it; I assumed it was the fever dream of a dying man. But when, with trembling hands, she dug out a purse of gold coins from the rags of her bed, a few thousand francs, I could no longer doubt.

You ask what could have induced one of society's high-ups to commit such a heinous offence. The reason is simple enough: if Molly was found to be alive, the vast estates of the Valricco family belonged to her; if she was dead, they belonged to the ambassador as his immediate heir.

My baby was alive! Any mother can understand the feelings that this news aroused in my chest. From that moment on, I had only one thought: I must get my baby back."

"I travelled to the family estate. For half a century, no child's body had been placed in the tomb of the old church. Marina's claim was confirmed.

I travelled to England and sought out Count Valricco. Our meeting turned into a fierce confrontation. He was cold, superior and sneering, declared me mad or an impostor, and threatened to have the valet throw me out or have the police take care of me. Except for me, I stated that I would never again accept a penny from his hands or live in the villa where I had experienced the happiest days of my life. So there I was, with only a few francs in my possession, alone without a home, without a livelihood, without protection. What was I to do? By chance, I saw a newspaper announcing that the Caruzzi circus was performing in Birmingham. I travelled there and returned to my former profession; I was not doing it just, or even mainly, for my livelihood; I wanted to raise funds to look for my lost daughter.

How these searches were conducted is not the point. While I was travelling around Europe, they never stopped. For a long time they produced no results; it was only nine months ago that I learnt that my Molly was at the Ingraham Institute in London.

It was at my insistence that Mr Caruzzi and his circus visited England. I knew that any attempt to get my child back peacefully was futile; I therefore devised a plan to abduct her from the Institute. It failed. I later learned that it was due to your intervention, Mr Holmes. And two days later, Molly was gone from the Institute - the Count had taken her himself. Where I never managed to find out.

So I stood once again at the starting point of my endeavours, hopeless, almost despairing. Then fate brought Debora Westrow into my path.

I found her sitting on the steps of the Ebenezer Chapel in Glover Street, exhausted, starving, homeless in the chill of the autumn evening. I was an unwitting cause of her plight - in my wanderings around the Institute, disguised as a man, I had spoken to her through the garden fence; it was crime enough for her to be thrown out into the world without protection or help. In the three days since she had been chased out, she had spent her last cent.

I recognised her and spoke to her; she told me of her sad fate, and I told her mine. The accident united us; we became friends, intimate friends, and from that moment, we had everything in common.

Her mind is sharper than mine, her knowledge greater. It was she who conceived the plan of taking employment in Count Valricco's house to seek some opportunity of getting on Molly's track or otherwise, to find some means of compelling the Count to give up the child. Yesterday fortune favoured her; she met the Count's dog with a paper in his mouth, snatched it from him without thinking of its great importance, but realised it as soon as she glanced at the letter. She is so perceptive, Deborah. And immediately, her mind was made up. She hid her find, left the service, arranged a meeting with me by telegraph and left me the letter.

There you have my story, Mr Holmes. Do you still call me a thief?"

During the latter part of the story, my friend began to pace up and down the room, a sign that his mind was working on a problem whose solution would not become clear. He stopped now and said, looking sharply at Flory:

"Are you telling the truth or lying, Miss?"

A flush of annoyance flushed across Flory's pretty face, but she controlled her emotion. "I have no right to be angry with you, sir, for you do not know me. To some extent I can prove the truth of my words." She went to a bureau and took out some papers: "Here is my marriage certificate, and here is little Molly's baptismal certificate; here are the two letters my beloved Alberto wrote to me during a fortnight's separation, the only one during our marriage when he travelled to the family estates. This is not very strong evidence for all I have said, but there is one more: Count Valricco's decision to agree to any conditions to get his letter back; he knows what I demand, and he is willing to give it. Is that not proof enough?"

Mr Holmes muttered something inaudible, then said aloud: "And what do you require to hand over the letter?"

"Just to get my baby back, my Molly. Everything else is unimportant to me. She may be called Nestle or White or Valricco; it doesn't matter to me."

"No, Miss White, or rather Countess Valricco, you must not act in this, may I say, thoughtless manner!" I exclaimed indignantly. My sense of justice would not allow me to be a mere indifferent listener, and Miss Flory was so delightful.

"The Count is a scoundrel, a criminal, and you have no right to give up little Molly's rights. I understand that she is to inherit the Valricco estate."

She smiled a ravishing smile at me and offered me her hand. "Thank you, doctor! You believe in me. It does me good; I am not used to such things nowadays. How can I thank you?"

The words and the handshake that followed were reward enough for me, and I was about to say so, when Sherlock Holmes interrupted: "I too believe in you, Countess Valricco! I have become an unwitting tool in the hands of a villain, but I will see to it that I am vindicated by getting you such. Countess, will you accept me as your helper?"

Flory looked at Holmes quizzically for a few moments before replying, "Yes, I do, Mr Holmes."

"I must make one condition: the letter must not be made public - even for the most important private interests, the peace of countries and states must not be jeopardised. Nor do I think it necessary; the Count will surely be amenable anyway."

I do not need to tell you what else was agreed before we parted late at night. The result can be seen in a couple of newspaper notices that I cut out and keep among my collections.

"A remarkable event. The niece of Count Valricco, the Albanian envoy to our Court, has for years been presumed dead, but has now been found alive in a girls' boarding house in Normandy. Success has thus at last crowned the many and costly searches for the missing girl conducted by the child's affectionate relative, Count Valricco, who has always, we know not on what grounds, doubted the child's death. The ambassador's action in this case is all the more commendable because he thereby loses the family's vast estates, which he had possessed, but which now pass to the child as the rightful owner."

That was the title of one newspaper article. The other, from a local newspaper, had the following content:

"The circus world has recently lost one of its most beautiful stars. We understand that Miss Flory White has left the ring, probably for good."

THE END

A story from

Yesteryear's stories reflected today
Yabot AB
www.yabot.se